Books by Isaac Bashevis Singer

NOVELS

The Manor [I. The Manor II. The Estate]
The Family Moskat • *The Magician of Lublin*
Satan in Goray • *The Slave*
Enemies, A Love Story • *Shosha*
The Penitent • *SCUM*

STORIES

Gimpel the Fool • *A Friend of Kafka* • *Short Friday*
The Séance • *The Spinoza of Market Street* • *Passions*
A Crown of Feathers • *Old Love* • *The Image*
The Death of Methuselah

MEMOIRS

In My Father's Court

FOR CHILDREN

A Day of Pleasure • *The Fools of Chelm*
Mazel and Shlimazel or The Milk of a Lioness
When Shlemiel Went to Warsaw
A Tale of Three Wishes • *Elijah the Slave*
Joseph and Koza or The Sacrifice to the Vistula
Alone in the Wild Forest • *The Wicked City*
Naftali the Storyteller and His Horse, Sus
Why Noah Chose the Dove
The Power of Light
The Golem

COLLECTIONS

The Collected Stories
Stories for Children
An Isaac Bashevis Singer Reader

SCUM

Flesh and corruption were the same from the very beginning,

and always will remain the scum of creation, the very opposite

of God's wisdom, mercy and splendor. . . Man would manage somehow

to crawl upon the surface of the earth, forward and backward,

until God's covenant with him ended and man's name in

the book of life was erased forever.

["The Death of Methuselah"]

SCUM

ISAAC BASHEVIS SINGER

Translated by Rosaline Dukalsky Schwartz

Farrar Straus Giroux

New York

SCUM

he Yiddish newspaper Max Barabander bought that morning in Warsaw carried the same news he had read in the papers in New York and London: the Balkan peninsula was a powder keg; Purishkevich, the notorious pogromist, and other members of the Black Hundreds were busily destroying Russian Jews; the Jewish colonies in Palestine were suffering from a drought; in Argentina bureaucrats of the Jewish Colonization Agency were again making trouble for Baron de Hirsch's colonies; Kaiser Wilhelm had aroused fresh bitterness in diplomatic circles with his belligerent threats; and the Zionists were preparing for a new congress. And in the news column entitled "The Four Corners of the Earth" there was an item about an Egyptian peasant woman who had given birth to six children, all dead.

Max Barabander read the paper while eating a cheese bun and sipping his coffee. "Six children at a crack!" he muttered to himself. "Will they dig six separate graves or will the children be buried in a single plot? And were they girls, or boys?"

On the ship bound from Argentina to England, and later in France and Germany, he could not obtain a Yiddish newspaper. He had bought a German paper in Berlin but the news in that foreign tongue lacked zest. In Yiddish every local story seemed to have its own flavor: a shoemaker bought a lottery ticket which would have won 75,000 rubles, but he had used it for toilet paper; a ship arrived in Australia carrying three hundred brides from England, chosen from photographs by the bridegrooms. Max gulped his coffee. "Three hundred girls! Damn their wicked little navels," he said to himself. "That's what I'd like, a ship with live merchandise." Max toyed with the idea: "Between a yes and a no, I'd make a million rubles."

He tapped the breast pocket where he kept his money, his Argentine passport, his return ticket, and his address book packed with names. He had been a thief himself and he had a deadly fear of being robbed. To reassure himself, he touched the gun in his coat pocket.

Max Barabander was forty-seven, but looked younger; people often took him for thirty-five or at most thirty-eight. He was tall, broad-shouldered, blond, with blue eyes, square chin, short neck, and straight nose. Even as a boy he was noted for his strength. When he struck a table with his fist, its legs splayed out like those of a slaughtered beast. He once made a bet he could eat three dozen eggs and drink twelve bottles of beer, and won the bet. What he could do with women no one, except the women involved, would believe. But as he approached fifty, the process of aging threw him into a panic; his hair had begun to thin and he could barely cover his bald spot.

Since his son, Arturo, had died, Max thought about death constantly. If a youth of seventeen can complain of a headache

and ten minutes later breathe his last, then man's existence is
not worth a puff of smoke. Somehow Max had forced himself
to put this calamity out of his mind, but his wife, Rochelle, had
become half-crazed. It was really because of her that he had
undertaken this journey. At home he could no longer endure
her ravings, which bordered on madness. She made Max say
Kaddish for their son, kept on lighting candles for Arturo's soul,
and gave frequent alms to charity. Her gallstone attacks were
so bad she had to undergo an operation. Max wanted to take
her to Poland after the doctors advised him that such a trip
would save her, but Rochelle insisted, "I must remain here with
Arturo."

The truth is that Max Barabander had recently extricated
himself from almost all his dirty business dealings. In fact, he
had become a part-owner of a Buenos Aires theater. When times
were right he had bought up dozens of houses and lots that now
brought in great profits. The newly arrived Jews in Argentina,
who were warring against the "unclean," would not allow them
into synagogue or permit them to buy burial grounds in the
cemetery. But Max remained on good terms with the community
leaders and even held the position of vice president of an or-
phanage. For years he had been leading a respectable life and
his marriage to Rochelle had satisfied him. Until the tragedy of
Arturo's death, she had been a ball of fire, taking him in hand
so completely that he had lost his taste for other women. But
Arturo's death changed everything: Rochelle had become cold,
she wouldn't let him near her; she wanted to die, continually
babbled of death, and had a monument maker engrave her own
tombstone. For the first time since Max had known her, she
sent him to other women. He had tried to do as she urged, but

he couldn't. This trip of Max's was for pleasure, not business. Now that he was in Poland, perhaps he would become rejuvenated.

On the ship he had heard all kinds of stories about South American pimps who kidnapped girls, dragging them off in carriages, selling respectable women into prostitution and forcing them to lead lives of shame. But Max had laughed at these farfetched stories; they may have done this sixty years ago, but nowadays it was impossible. Anyway, you could always get girls to make the journey willingly. Max knew he had really come to Poland looking for a girlfriend. He also knew that Rochelle would never again revert to what she had been. If he was to remain a man, he would have to feel desire for a woman as strongly as he had once desired Rochelle.

He had several other matters to settle in Poland. Years earlier, he had abandoned his father and mother in Roszkow, had never written them a line, and they had died without knowing what had become of him. Somewhere in Poland he had a brother, Zalmen, and a sister, Sore-Nekhe, not to mention uncles, aunts, and cousins. He also still had good friends in Poland. But how could he show up in front of relatives and friends after twenty-three years of silence? And could he visit his parents' graves in the cemetery when he had perhaps been to blame for their deaths?

Max took a last gulp of coffee and swallowed the last bite of his cheese bun. Only an hour ago he had arrived by express from Berlin, leaving his luggage in the baggage room of the Vienna Station. Walking the streets of Warsaw, he went as far as the Grzybow district. He knew the city well, having lived there through good times and bad. He had even spent three months in the Powiak prison, but that was twenty years ago.

In those days a horse-drawn trolley had just begun to operate in Warsaw; now in 1906 they had electric trolley cars and from time to time an automobile drove by. He noticed that the stores on Marszalkowska Street were displaying fine merchandise and that women now dressed no less fashionably than those in Paris and Berlin. The streets were wider and the buildings higher. Though the Jewish quarter had changed less, even here one got the feeling of new times, of the twentieth century. Many younger men shaved off their beards and wore hats and suits; young Jewish women wore short-sleeved dresses, cut so that one could see their bare necks. When Max had lived there previously, all Jewish girls wore shawls, hats were a rarity, and handbags unknown.

The newspaper now carried announcements of Yiddish plays, a poetry reading in Hazomir, an evening of song with Shneyer's choir, a meeting of students at the center. Doctors even advertised that they could cure venereal disease and "men's troubles."

"Well, the world has progressed a little," Max murmured. How strange! Among the people in the café were several girls who sat at small tables eating breakfast and looking at newspapers. What kind of girls are they? Max wondered. In Argentina you never saw a decent girl sitting alone, especially in a restaurant. But these Fräuleins appeared to be respectable; from the way they dressed, they appeared to be factory workers or shop girls.

While living abroad, Max had read about Russia's 1905 revolution and the war between the underworld and the workers—or rather, the strikers. Emigrés brought over all kinds of stories about Bloody Sunday, the bomb that Boruch Shulman threw at the police, the demonstrations, the strikes, the mass arrests, and how the Tsar had finally given in and allowed Russia to have a Duma or national assembly. But one columnist claimed that everything was exactly the same: power was still in the hands of the Black Hundreds and old Rasputin had hypnotized the Tsar, the Tsarina, and the ladies of the court.

"Where do I go now?" Max Barabander asked himself. He pulled out his address book, leafing through it, and saw the name Hotel Bristol, which he remembered from the past. People used to say that generals and merchants from the First Guild stayed there, and if anyone in prison complained that his bed was too hard, the fellows would wisecrack, "Tomorrow they'll move you to the Hotel Bristol." Well, Max Barabander would be staying there now.

He went outside, called a droshky, and asked to be driven to the Vienna Station. He reclaimed his two leather valises from the baggage room and a porter carried them to the waiting droshky. Max gave him ten kopecks and the porter bowed.

"Yes, with money in hand one is the lord of the land," Max mused to himself. "Whoever can pay has the say."

He leaned his head against the side of the coach and inhaled deeply. Every city has its own smell. His nose remembered the odor of Warsaw from the past as a mixture of lilacs, sewage, tar, winds sweeping in from the Praga forests, and a something that had no name. As for the noise, the trolleys clanged differently and the wheels of the carriages clattered differently over the cobblestones. A din still arose from the marketplace and from the voices of cheder boys who were reciting the Pentateuch aloud. The droshky stopped at the Hotel Bristol and a porter carried Max's valises up the marble stairs.

"A room, like other rooms," Max muttered to himself, touching the mattress with a practiced hand. "Not bad. All that's

missing is a woman." He sat in an armchair and lit a cigarette.
Again he took out his address book. You have to begin somewhere; one acquaintance would lead to another.

I wonder what Rochelle is doing in Argentina now, he
thought. Here in Poland it's summer, but there it's winter. Here
when it's night, there it's day. Seas, rivers, and countries separated him from Rochelle, but what was it that continued to
bind him to her? Only thought and memory.

In his own way Max Barabander was a philosopher who
pondered over all sorts of ideas. He did not believe in the
Pentateuch but felt that God was present in the Talmud. Every
person has his destiny. But why? Why does the world need a
Kaiser Wilhelm, a Purishkevich, or a Blind Mayer? The friend
who had suggested he look up Blind Mayer did not know his
address but told Max to visit the tavern on Krochmalna Street.

Blind Mayer was the leader of the local hoodlums, a sort
of rabbi of the tough guys. Max really had no intention of getting
mixed up with the Warsaw underworld. Why would anyone of
sound mind get into a sickbed? But taking a look around couldn't
hurt. Max had once lived on Krochmalna Street and remembered the tavern quite well.

His gold watch showed seven o'clock, but it still seemed
like the middle of the day. Summer days in Warsaw are longer
than in Buenos Aires or New York; it doesn't get dark until
close to ten. This time Max did not take a droshky but walked.
First he went to Gnoyna Street and looked around. The same
smells of oil, soap, and herring. A janitor with a tin badge on
his hat was sweeping up horse droppings. Standing around in
the shops were heavily bearded Jews in long gaberdine coats,

wearing thick boots. Why aren't they hot? Max wondered, having himself put on a light suit and a straw hat.

He turned into Krochmalna Street. On one side there was a high fence, on the other side a building without windows. "What is it—a factory, an armory?" He walked along and soon came to the square, the famous meeting place of thieves, swindlers, pimps, whores. Everything was the same. Young boys with caps pulled down over their eyes were standing in groups, talking, and whispering. A bunch of young fellows were playing in the lottery; they picked numbers out of a bag, spun a wooden rooster, and won a *tchaste*, a pastry baked in oil and covered with chocolate. Streetwalkers lurked by the gates and Max looked at them with a practiced eye. They didn't use rouge but seemed to have rubbed their faces with red paper; they wore loose silk dresses, red stockings, and yellow sandals. One was small and round as a tub, the other pockmarked, with sunken cheeks and a forehead covered with pimples. You have to be hard up to want one of them, Max thought. The smell of smoke and baked goods pervaded the air and a stench that Max had long since forgotten assailed him.

Two young hoodlums spotted him, winked at each other, drifted over to him, and one asked, "Uncle, where are you from?"

"I am not your uncle, so get lost," Max answered.

"A big shot, huh?"

"Yes! Beat it or else you'll get one right in the kisser."

"A tough guy, hey?"

Max wasn't afraid of this kind of riffraff, but he realized it didn't pay to get into a fight. He pushed past them and strode on.

Nothing has changed here, Max thought. The same filth, the same poverty. Peddler women sat in the marketplace selling rotten fruit, onions without skins, cracked eggs they called "little wrinkles," and darned stockings. Old women dressed in caps and padded clothes, as if it were still winter, called out, "Hot chick peas! Beans! Potato cakes!"

I'll just take a look and never come back here again, Max decided. When he arrived at No. 6, he opened the saloon door and stood looking in. Some young men were sitting at tables playing dominoes, while others were dealing out decks of soiled cards; a few were standing at the bar talking to a short, heavily freckled girl with full lips. Flies were crawling over the cakes and pastries that lay on the counter. Could this be the place where Blind Mayer is a regular? Max wondered.

Someone called out: "Hey there, Freemason, close the door!"

"Come in but watch out," a girl kidded him. Max pulled back, closed the door, and moved on. He had no intention of staying in such a suffocating place on a hot day. He walked on to No. 17 and, recognizing the tavern, opened the door. It was much more orderly here. The floor was tiled in black-and-white squares. The bar held trays of roasted geese, bowls of chopped herring, jellied calves' feet, and baskets with salt rolls, as well as plates of egg cookies. A heavyset fellow drew beer from a tap into mugs. Men and women were sitting at tables, drinking, talking, and nibbling on appetizers. Max found an empty table, sat down, and ordered a beer from the waiter.

"Bavarian or Avshane?" the waiter asked. The names sounded familiar to Max, but he had forgotten what they were. He smiled. "Just a cold beer."

"Something with it—chopped herring? Chopped liver? Cold cuts?"

Max thought it over. "Make it chopped herring with rye bread."

He looked around. Having been born and raised in poverty, he couldn't stand squalor. Rochelle, who had lived through hard times, quickly got used to luxury, loved beautiful clothes, expensive furniture, and the finest jewelry. She enjoyed gambling in casinos and went on trips with him to Rio de Janeiro and New York. Though Max himself had never learned to speak Spanish properly, Rochelle spoke it fluently and Arturo like a native. Their son had been sent to schools catering to wealthy families. Rochelle had also proved to be an astute businesswoman and he never made a business deal without consulting her.

But the seven good years had passed. Rochelle was now a broken woman and Max, the great womanizer, was impotent. In Paris he had engaged the services of a beautiful girl. He took a trip with her to Deauville, where they stayed in the best hotel. But as soon as she embraced him, he was overcome by sadness and disgust and suddenly felt like throwing up. Neither the champagne nor her seductive snares helped. The same thing had happened to him in Berlin and even on the ship. He had consulted doctors in America and Europe, and they all said the same thing: nerves. They prescribed hydropathy, warm baths and medicines that were as effective as cupping a corpse. They all gave the same advice: Take a long trip, forget your misfortunes, find fresh companionship and new interests.

The waiter brought a mug of beer, bread with chopped herring, a sour pickle, and, on the house, a bowl of peppered peas. Max waited for the foam to settle, then downed half a mug in one gulp and munched on the chopped herring. The pleasure of eating was all that was left him. He seldom got drunk and avoided the company drunkards with their empty talk, boasting, and whining. Max often thought that, despite his forty-seven years, he was still young at heart, with a young man's fantasies. Even though he was rich, in his dreams he still made millions, found hidden treasures, courted opera singers, great ladies, and princesses who fell in love with him. He not only became as rich as Rothschild but advanced loans to the Tsar of Russia and purchased Palestine from the Sultan.

Max had read of Dr. Theodor Herzl, who died of a heart attack because he could not secure Palestine for the Jewish people. Every year Max contributed a shekel in support of the Zionist cause. He even planned to visit Palestine on his return trip: see Jerusalem, the grave of Rachel, the Wailing Wall, and the colonies where young people, free-thinkers and ex-students, plowed the earth, planted vineyards, and spoke Hebrew.

Yes, here in the building at No. 17 Max had once lived in a garret, passing the tavern every day. He had never gone in because in those days he could not afford a glass of beer. At one point he was in a lot of trouble for thievery and the police were looking for him. He was finally arrested and served his time in the Powiak prison. Now he was a citizen of the Republic of Argentina and his passport was stamped with a Russian visa. No one could touch him.

Sitting alone at a table in a tavern was a dubious pleasure. If only Rochelle were with him! If only he could find another woman with whom he could be close. He looked around. The few women sitting at the tables were middle-aged, fat and fleshy, and looked like shopkeepers from Yanush's Court. They spoke in hoarse voices, and one woman wore an apron with wide pockets like a peddler's. No, this was not what Max was looking for. Taking out his address book and thumbing through the pages again, he found a name and address and could not remember who had given it to him. Traveling had unhinged his memory: he kept losing his glasses, misplacing the fountain pens he had bought in New York, and when he changed his suit he forgot to remove his money, his papers, and his handkerchief.

New patrons were coming in, but no one looked at him. They all seemed to know each other and pushed their tables together, talking loudly, laughing, and drinking toasts to a long life. Their leader was a man with a big belly, a straight neck, and a heavy face whose vest was draped with a chain of golden five-ruble pieces. They called him Shmuel, laughed at his jokes, and played up to him. Whinnying and wheezing like an asthma sufferer, he spoke in a voice peculiar to people with enlarged hearts. He looked as if he had once been a giant, but Max was certain that such a man could suffer a stroke at any moment. The fat man poured himself one mug of beer after another, snacking on tripe and mashed potatoes.

Max overheard him telling how he had rescued an assistant rabbi from going to jail. This good man had performed a marriage against the law, because an assistant rabbi did not have official government permission to marry anyone. He could have been sentenced from three months to a year in prison, but he, Shmuel, had gone to the investigating judge and fixed it. A heavy woman with flaccid, loose-fleshed arms, a gigantic balcony of a bosom, and a head that became increasingly wider said in a rasping voice, "He let himself be greased, huh?"

"Without grease, the wheels don't turn. The good man came to my home pleading, 'Mr. Shmuel, save me.' He was shivering. I was afraid he'd pass out right in my house. Three days in the clinker and a man like that is gone."

"We give him a weekly allotment."

"He's got four children."

"The rabbi's wife buys fish from me for the Sabbath," the heavy woman said, "three-quarters of a pound. Don't say anything, but I add to the weight—call it my good deed."

"She once ordered a raw silk wig from me," said another woman.

"What kind of stuff is that?"

"You don't know? Not hair, but silk."

"A rebbetzin is not supposed to wear someone else's hair."

"Why not?"

"If a man sees hair, he starts to get horny."

There was an outburst of laughter and thumping. The heavy woman blew her nose into her apron and Shmuel banged his fist on the table. "Don't laugh. We live on their merits."

Max Barabander could hold back no longer. He rose, went to their table, and said, "I hear you speaking the mother tongue. May I sit down? I'm not from this country, I've just come from overseas."

"An American, huh?"

"Argentina is also in America."

They became quiet and Shmuel spoke up: "Well, pull up your chair. Where do you come from, Buenos Aires?"

"From Buenos Aires, from New York, from Paris—from the whole world."

"Well, what's happening out there in that big world?" Shmuel asked.

"It's a big world with many little worlds," Max answered,

not sure himself what he was going to say next. "In Buenos Aires if you want to say that you are earning a living, the expression is "You make America." In New York, you make a living. In London if you ask a Jew how he's doing, he'll say it could be a lot better, and in Paris they forget altogether that they are Jews. They sit in cafés and for ten centimes stay there from morning till night. If you tell them something, they say 'Oo la la,' and ask you to treat them to an aperitif. That's a glass of wine. You can drink ten glasses and never get drunk."

"They don't drink any hard liquor?" Shmuel asked.

"The French prefer wine, which is good for a benediction, not to quicken the heart," Max said. "Can I set up some brandy?" he asked.

"What do you mean by 'set up'?"

"Order for the whole table."

"We're not beggars, we can order our own brandy, but if you want to drink for friendship, so to speak, by all means. As my grandfather used to say, Never pass up a glass of brandy or a pinch of snuff."

"What do you want to eat with it?"

"In what holy book is it written that one must eat something with it?"

"I'll take a side order of tripe," the heavy-looking market woman called out.

"What's the matter, Reytsele, you're not fat enough?" Shmuel kidded her.

"My husband likes me just the way I am."

"This tough cookie can stand up for herself," Shmuel commented. "What did you say your name was, hm?"

"Max Barabander."

"My name is Shmuel Vakhler, but they call me Shmuel Smetena. They gave me that name and it stuck."

"Why Smetena? You like sour cream?"

"I like everything that others don't dislike. That's why I have such a big belly. Is it true that they snatch girls off the streets and carry them away to Argentina?"

"They go there by themselves."

"Here's the waiter . . ." Some ordered ordinary brandy, others wanted cognac, and Max ordered whiskey. The waiter shrugged, not knowing what whiskey was. Max had used the word to show he was a foreigner and knew drinks they had never heard of.

Besides Shmuel Smetena and Reytsele, three other women and two men had joined the table. One short, broad, and square-faced man, almost without a neck, had pushed a cap over his blond hair. They called him Zelig, and Shmuel Smetena said that on the street he was known as Zelig Kishke or Zelig Fischer. Mahkle, Zelig's wife, a chubby little woman with a crooked nose and yellow eyes set very close to each other, smiled and darted glances at Shmuel Smetena and at Max. From time to time it seemed to Max that she was winking at him. What's wrong with her? Does she still think of herself as a desirable woman? Max wondered.

He noticed a thin man, all skin and bones, whose skull lacked a single hair. He was dressed like an aristocrat in a striped suit, a stiff collar, a dickey, and a tie and pin. His lapel held the kind of paper flower that is sold by charitable societies. Speaking in the thin voice of a weak man, he ordered ninety-proof brandy with a hot sausage.

"What is the flower for?"

"It's from the Health Society."

"What's that?"

"They send people with tuberculosis away to Otwock."

"And what happens there?"

"That's their last stop. Soon they're packed up in travel trunks."

"You should be ashamed of yourself, Fulye, the way you talk!" the little woman exclaimed.

"But it's the truth!"

"For the truth you get a beating," Shmuel Smetena replied.

"*L'chaim!*" Max drank his whiskey and munched on some jellied calves' feet cooked in onions and garlic. He was suffused with a joy he had not felt for a long time.

Neither Paris nor Berlin had provided the right company. There they used French or German expressions or spoke in the Lithuanian Yiddish dialect. Besides, almost everyone he encountered abroad was younger than he and treated him like an old man. You can never tell where you might find a friendly face. Less than half an hour in this tavern and already these people were calling him Max. One of the regulars, an older man named Haym Kaviornik, revealed that he owned a coffeehouse not far away, at No. 8. "If you like cheese buns come over to my place. You can't get better cheese buns in the whole world," he said.

"What do they eat in Argentina?" a woman who had been silent asked Max. She was forty or more, small and dark, with bobbed hair already flecked with gray. Her eyes, which were as dark as black cherries, were underlined with wrinkles. She had a short nose, a small chin, and her eyebrows met. She seemed more refined than the others, and though not young she had a girlish look. When she smiled, her small, widely spaced teeth showed white and a dimple appeared in her left cheek. Max looked at her several times but she somehow avoided his gaze. She was wearing a gray jacket with the kind of purse belted over it in which shopkeepers put their cash.

Max felt restored. "I thought you were dumb," he said to her.

Shmuel let out a whinnying laugh. "Just start up with her and you'll hear language that will burn your ears."

"Why should I start up with her? What we eat in Argentina is beefsteak, twice a day. We ship beef all over the world. We have a kind of grass called alfalfa, and when the cattle eat it they get very fat. You can travel hundreds of miles in Argentina and all you will see are the pampas—grass and cattle."

"In Argentina they may export cattle meat but they import human flesh," Shmuel wisecracked.

"That's true, but soon they won't have to bother importing. The Spanish woman is not exactly virtuous. The trouble is, you just look at her and she gets pregnant."

"From a mere look?" the woman with the black eyes asked.

"That's what they say. In Argentina, the non-Jews—the men, that is—are not observant. Even on Sunday they don't go to church. The whole shmoliness lies with the señoras. They go to church, make their confessions to the priest, and so on. And when the lady's husband isn't at home, you can have your way with her. But she doesn't last long—by the age of thirty she's finished. That's what the climate does. Besides, almost every man there has a mistress."

"A wonderful country."

"A place where the blood runs hot. People say bad things about Argentina, but if you went there you would understand. You get an urge and must act on it right away."

"How come you left such a wonderful country and came all the way to Krochmalna Street?" the little woman asked.

"There is a reason for everything. Are you a shopkeeper?"

"My husband's a baker and I sell bread, rolls, and bagels. We have a place at No. 15 Krochmalna Street."

"What's your name?"

"Esther."

"Selling bread's a good living. People always want to eat bread and rolls."

"My husband has twelve apprentices. How long are you staying in Warsaw?"

"I don't know."

"Come around tomorrow night. We eat supper about ten o'clock. I'll introduce you to my sister. She's about ten years younger than me."

"You're not so old either."

"Not so old and not so young—a grandmother. I have a two-year-old grandchild. And where are you staying in War-saw?"

"At the Hotel Bristol."

There was moment's silence. "You can't be a poor person," Shmuel Smetena said.

"Poor people don't come to Poland to visit their parents' graves," said Max Barabander, surprised at his own words.

"Well then, you are one of us," said Shmuel. "Here in Warsaw you don't get rich. Without a rich father, you can't become a wealthy man. In other countries, in America, you work your way up. What's your line of work, huh?"

"Houses and lots."

"And you really came to visit your parents' graves?"

"My parents are buried in Roszkow."

"Where is that? I thought you were from Warsaw."

"I once lived here, right in No. 17."

"Americans come and you can barely understand their speech. A man of sixty comes here and he looks like forty. He runs after the young girls and all of sudden he gets sick and has to go to the hospital. One thing they do have is dollars. For one dollar you get two rubles. What kind of money do they use in Argentina?"

"The peso."

"When people come here they say it feels like home. Once a man from London showed up and drove over to Falenicz with us. In London, he said, there's no clean air—it's all smoke and the sun doesn't shine. Every day there's a fog, and it rains, too. There money is weighed by the pound or the Devil knows what. But one thing is the same everywhere—you have to hand out bribes constantly. If you have a store and are forced to close it at seven o'clock in the evening, how can you afford to lock up just at seven when everyone comes home from work and goes shopping? So you have to pay off the policeman or his sergeant. If not, he'll report you and you'll have your hands full. That's my job. You have to know who to give to and how. You can't just take out three rubles and hand them to the commissar. He'll arrest you on the spot for offering a bribe, and for that you can go to the slammer.

"With some you have to play cards, Oke or Sixty-six, and lose," Shmuel continued. "Otherwise they don't take the bribe. When Shmuel Smetena telephones that he wants to play a game of cards, the big chief knows he'll win, even if he has the worst hand. Once I had two nines—we call them *shragess*, worthless cards—and two jacks. With cards like that, you have to get out right away. But I really don't come to play cards. Knowing that the vice-commissar had four aces, I bet five rubles for my first hand, and when he put down twenty-five, I lost. Usually when they win, they don't bother to look at your cards; but this time he stretched out his paw and took a look. 'You devil, you wanted to scare me, ha?' And I said, 'Yes, Your Excellency.' That's how it is with us. You can play cards with Stolypin or with the Tsar himself if you're ready to lose a big enough sum."

"Esther," Shmuel said, turning to the baker woman, "your husband is a baker, not a smuggler, but he gives bribes, too. Their wives come and get baked goods for nothing. Is that true or not?"

"You're discovering America?"

"What sins does a baker commit?" Max asked.

Esther smiled. "In the eyes of the Russian pig everything is a sin. They send health inspectors around who claim the bakery's not clean. In their barracks they knead dough with their feet, but by us it's not clean. Come around to my place tomorrow night. My husband will tell you everything." The little woman averted her eyes.

"Your husband bakes bagels until eleven at night," Shmuel said.

"By ten he's already at home."

"Don't play games, Esther. What are you carrying on about? Invite this man to your house. You can go to her, Max. Her cooking is fit for a king. She has a good-looking sister and a beautiful daughter, and she's not poison either." Everyone laughed and Esther blushed like a young girl.

"Shmuel, you are talking nonsense. I'm already a grand-mother."

*   *   *

After everyone had left, Max remained alone to pay the bill and then went outside. Usually summer evenings turn cool, but not here. Heat radiated from the brick walls, the tin roofs, the cobblestones. The street swarmed with boys and girls who played in the middle of the street and when a droshky came by waited until the last possible moment to step aside.

Max set out again for Gnoyna Street. At every courtyard gate streetwalkers called out to the men. Max, who had been drinking steadily, was a little high but his mood was subdued. Why had he made this long journey—to talk to Shmuel Smetena? To be invited to the house of a baker's wife who was a grandmother? Although he once had many girlfriends in Warsaw, he no longer knew where they lived.

Why don't I just go to Roszkow? Max thought. I might actually do something worthwhile. A man doesn't live forever.

For a while he tried to picture what would happen if he suddenly dropped dead here. Rochelle would probably never know where his bones were laid to rest. What was it that his mother (may she rest in peace) used to say? "Life is a dance on graves." What should he do? Have a scribe prepare a Torah scroll? Give his money to a health society that sells paper flowers?

He suddenly remembered the good man, the rabbi that Shmuel Smetena had saved from going to prison. Perhaps he could go to see him and give him a few rubles. It wasn't so late, nobody had gone to sleep yet. Max Barabander realized his impulse was a piece of insanity. Was he suddenly going to become a philanthropist? He was—God forbid—not sick, but somehow a force was driving him.

He stopped an old woman in a cap. "What do you want?" she asked.

"Where does the rabbi live? I've forgotten his name. A good man. People go to him to get married."

"You mean the assistant rabbi? He's in No. 10, on the first floor. You see the balcony, where it's lit?"

"Many thanks."

"To the left of the gate."

Max crossed the street and went through the gate where a tiny kerosene lamp glimmered. He stood for a while and looked into the courtyard. In the light that fell from the windows he saw a garbage bin, a blank wall, and an outhouse. It was getting late but people were still at work. Max could hear the whirr of sewing machines, the tapping of shoemakers' hammers, a clatter and a hum as if he were in a factory.

He had forgotten that there were cellar apartments. His glance took in an apartment to the left with a crooked ceiling and a small window touching the earth. Laundry hung on lines. A housewife was making up a bed on a wide bench. In the kitchen a girl was boiling a pot of potatoes. Max thought about giving them a few rubles, but he would have to crawl down those dark stairs. He realized the stairs that led up to the rabbi's house were also unlit.

"Ah, they live like a hundred years ago," he said to himself as he walked up the stairs.

He was wondering which door to knock on when one of them opened by itself and he saw a kitchen with walls painted pink. There were pots on the brick-tiled oven, and a kerosene lamp with a tin shade hung from the ceiling. A woman sat at the table writing.

"Where does the good man live?" asked Max Barabander. "I mean the . . ."

The woman lifted her bewigged head. She had a narrow

face, sunken cheeks, and a small nose. Her gray eyes gave him a questioning look, a bit frightened, yet with a restrained smile.

"You want to see the assistant rabbi?"

"Yes, the assistant rabbi."

"My husband is the assistant rabbi, but he's not at home now. Do you need to ask him a question?"

"Mm, not a question."

"My husband is downstairs in the prayerhouse. The Neustadter prayerhouse, that's what it's called."

"You're the rebbetzin, then?"

"Yes, the rebbetzin."

"Come in and close the door, if you will," said a young woman who was sitting on the bed. Her tone of voice carried a hint of impatience and mockery. Max observed that she was about eighteen or nineteen, wearing a calico dress with a high collar and long sleeves, with dark hair twisted into a bun. Her face shone brightly even though she was in a shadow. There was something about her that perplexed Max. She seemed both provincial and cosmopolitan, almost like the ladies he had seen in Paris and Berlin. Her beauty stood out because another girl—her sister?—sitting on a trunk with a shawl draped over her shoulders was dark-skinned with a wide nose and heavy, mannish eyebrows. Max closed the door behind him and stood for a moment, not knowing what to say. As usual, he let his tongue do the talking.

"I've come from far-off lands. I went into the tavern at No. 17 and a certain Shmuel Smetena told me about your husband. You are surely his daughter," he said, turning to the fairer one. "Or are you sisters? He spoke about the rabbi having—how shall I say—trouble over a wedding. Don't be afraid, I'm not a spy. I heard that the good man was suffering and it occurred to me that he must have a very hard time eking out a living. I once had parents here but they died. Not here in Warsaw, but in Roszkow. That's a town in the province of Lublin. You may perhaps know where it is. I came to visit my parents' graves. I'm from Warsaw, too, originally. I lived here over twenty years ago."

Everyone's eyes were on him in wonder. The rebbetzin gave him a penetrating look. The fair girl's eyes were filled with laughter and the dark, heavy one stared in openmouthed bewilderment. The rebbetzin laid down her pen. "Wait a moment. My husband will come soon. Tsirele, bring in a chair for our guest."

Tsirele, the fair one, got up hesitantly. She opened the door to an unlit room and brought in a chair. She placed it in the middle of the room.

"Thanks," Max said. "I don't have to sit. My mother used to say, 'One should only be able to stand well.' I sat for a day and a half in the train. Although I went second-class, it got tiresome. Here I'm staying at the Hotel Bristol."

"At the Hotel Bristol?" Tsirele exclaimed. "That must cost a fortune!"

"It's not a fortune, four rubles a day."

"That's twenty-eight rubles a week!"

"What of it? In Berlin I paid twelve marks a day. That's six rubles."

"You must be a millionaire."

"Tsirele, don't talk nonsense," the rebbetzin intervened. "If the Lord helps . . ."

"Six rubles a day is forty-two rubles a week. Where do you get such money? Where do you live—in America?"

"Yes, in South America."

"We've been sitting here and dreaming of hiring a teacher," said Tsirele. "We want to learn Russian and Polish, too. Yesterday a teacher came here who wants twenty kopecks a lesson. Three lessons a week is sixty kopecks, four gulden. He would teach both of us for that rate. But where do you get so much money? This is my friend Leahtche," Tsirele said, pointing to the other girl.

"Leahtche, huh? I had a cousin Leah. She died of smallpox thirty years ago, may that never happen to you."

"They didn't vaccinate against smallpox then?" the rebbetzin asked.

"Not in Roszkow. You live here on this street, too?" Max asked Leah. She looked as if she was about to answer but the words took a long time to come out of her mouth. And when they did they were uttered with the exertion of a stammerer. "We live on a humble street," she said. "We come from Wyszkow. First my father came, then my mother with my brother Yoyl and my sister Nemi and my youngest sister."

"What does your father do? Is he also an assistant rabbi?"

Leah's face broke out in a smile. "Oh, he is a matchmaker and peddles watches on the side. My older brother is a clerk in an office."

"Since your father is a matchmaker, why doesn't he arrange a match for you?"

The rebbetzin frowned. "She is still a young girl. When the time comes, she will surely find her intended."

"I've come here and somehow everything seems strange. I've been out in the wide world for over twenty years and suddenly I'm back here again! I was in the tavern and Shmuel Smetena told the whole story. What does it matter to the Russian pig if a good man performs the marriage ceremony? And then everyone left the tavern. But a hotel is not a home, no matter how grand it is. And as people say, being alone is depressing. So it occurred to me to come and see the good man."

"Do you have a family in that America?" the rebbetzin asked.

"Had."

"What happened?"

"I had a son, Arturo, that's what he was called. My wife named him after her father, Arye Leyb. In Argentina Arye becomes Arturo. A lovely child, clever and handsome. Came home from a walk and said that he had a headache. My wife told him to rest on the bed. He lay down and gave a sigh. My wife went to get him a glass of water and when she came back it was all over."

The rebbetzin winced. "God save and protect us!"

"I couldn't stay home anymore," said Max.

"How is your wife?"

"My wife passed away after him," Max heard himself say, astonished at his own words.

"God save us! What happened, did she become ill?"

"She took poison."

The rebbetzin wrung her slender hands. She bent her head as if to spit, but didn't. "May we all be shielded from such sorrow. Surely she lost her mind out of pain. May the Lord on High forgive her!"

"One day I had a home and suddenly I was stripped of my family."

There was silence for a while and the wick could be heard sucking up the kerosene in the lamp.

"What do you do?"

"Sell houses and lots."

"Well, everything is ordained. Nothing happens at random," the rebbetzin said sternly.

It suddenly occurred to Max that the rebbetzin was wearing the same kind of wig that the hairdresser had spoken about in the tavern, a wig made with raw silk. He wanted to ask about it but realized this was not the right time. He had invented a wild lie! For what reason?

Tsirele inclined her head to one side. She regarded him warily and penetratingly but with curiosity. She suddenly said, "In that case, you have made this trip to forget your *verzweiflung*."

It had been a long time since Max had heard this Germanic-Yiddish word for despair, one of those words that appear in newspapers. But nevertheless he understood its meaning and it stung him, tore at his guts. This fledgling, the rabbi's daughter, had expressed in one word what was wrong with him and why he had made this journey. A shiver ran down his spine.

"Yes, that's why." He had to change the subject. "What are you writing, Rebbetzin?" Max asked.

"Receipts."

"What are they for? The shul?"

"My husband doesn't belong to the rabbinate and is not given any money by the community. The street provides him with a weekly allotment. A collector makes the rounds, gathering contributions, and he gives everyone a receipt."

"And from this the good man lives?"

"Sometimes a wedding comes along, a divorce, a lawsuit."

Max thought for a while. "A pious man should have enough to live on so that he can study Torah and not have to worry about money."

Tsirele laughed and her eyes sparkled. "There are many things that should be. In our street there are porters who carry such heavy loads on their backs it's a wonder they don't collapse under their burdens. Most of them are older Jews. I once saw one of them carrying a whole wardrobe. Why he did not collapse under its weight I will never know. And where do these people live? In dark cellar rooms where it's so damp that they will undoubtedly come down with consumption. They wear rags and tatters. Recently one of them died and people put together money for a shroud."

"Tsirele, don't mix in the porters when we are talking about your father," the rebbetzin protested. "Of course those Jews are to be pitied. But one thing doesn't have anything to do with the other."

"Yes it does, Mama. In a righteous world no one will suffer need and in an unrighteous one all suffer except for a few exploiters and bloodsuckers."

"The strikers smashed your father's windows."

"A few foolish boys. They were vexed that Father spoke up against them in the prayerhouse. Why should one pauper speak out against another? They weren't battling against Father but against the Tsar."

The rebbetzin shuddered and put down her pen. "Daughter! What are you saying? Your talk will bring us to the gallows."

"Don't be afraid, Mama. This man is not an informer."

"God forbid. But walls have ears. The Tsar can't make everyone rich. If the Tsar divided up all his wealth it would amount to a three-ruble note for each person."

"No one is asking him to share the wealth. Let him give the people freedom, real freedom, not a Duma where they are afraid to utter a word because the secret police are in control through their spies . . ."

"Daughter, will you keep quiet or not?" The rebbetzin

raised her voice. "A person comes in and she starts right in with her arguments. We cannot take care of the whole world. There always were poor people and there always will be, unless the Messiah comes. It says in the Torah: 'There will never cease to be poor people on this earth.' "

"I know, Mama, I know. How could our teacher Moses know what would happen three thousand years later? We don't have to have poor people. There is enough grain in Russia for everyone to eat his fill. Russia even exports grain to other lands. We can build factories where everything is manufactured—clothing, shoes, whatever a person needs. Instead, the peasants go barefoot and naked. And a piece of bread is a luxury for those who till the soil and harvest the grain for the bread that others eat. They don't give their children the barest education. And if they teach them anything, it is to kiss the cross."

"So you are going to take care of the peasants when they are anti-Semites and make pogroms against the Jews?"

"They make pogroms because the Black Hundreds instigate them. What do the peasants have against the Jewish workers in Berdichev or Kishinev? Purishkevich incites them and they follow like sheep. Someone has to come and tell them the truth."

"So run and tell them!"

"If only I knew Russian."

Max looked on in amazement. He had never heard a girl talk like this. Tsirele's girlfriend Leahtche sat openmouthed, her chin reminding Max of a cow's jaw.

"Rebbetzin, don't be angry with her," Max said. "She has a brain and she thinks. It's because her father is a rabbi and—how does the saying go?—the apple doesn't fall far from the tree. He thinks about the Torah and she wants it to have results. In America there are also socialists and they feel free to demonstrate. On the first of May they carry red flags and all the rest. They strive for shorter working hours and better pay."

"There they don't have a Tsar and they still have poor people," the rebbetzin said. "Who sweeps the chimneys, Rockefeller?"

"How do you know about Rockefeller, Rebbetzin?"

"We know. My daughter buys a newspaper every day and reads it thoroughly. You can't take care of the whole world!" The rebbetzin's tone of voice changed. "The Almighty created the world and oversees it. Better go wash the dishes."

"Not now, Mama, not now."

"Rebbetzin, don't be angry with me," Max began, not knowing what he was about to say. "I was sitting in the tavern and overheard people talking about the rabbi and I would like, as you might say, to do something. I myself am not a poor man. But what do I get out of my money? I would like to go downstairs and buy something. It will be my good deed. The shops are open and you can get everything—sausages, fresh rolls, bagels, sardines. Perhaps you'd like a glass of wine or brandy? It's good for the appetite. The good man will come back from shul soon and he, too, will want to have a bite to eat."

The rebbetzin knit her brows. "We are not rich people but, praised be His Name, we have enough to eat. Thank you for your good heart, but it is not necessary."

"Perhaps I can contribute something toward a religious book or some holy object?"

"My husband will come soon and he—"

As the rebbetzin spoke, footsteps were heard on the stairs. Tsirele managed to laugh and wink at the same time. The steps were heavy and hasty. The door opened and Max saw the rabbi, a short, somewhat broad man, wearing a long gaberdine coat down to his ankles, heavy boots, and a hat that was worn and tattered. He had a red beard, dark curly sidelocks, a white face, a short nose, and light eyes.

"He and his daughter are as alike as two drops of water," Max said to himself. An extraordinary warmth radiated from this man. Max somehow had the feeling that he had met him before.

The rabbi apparently wanted to say something. He had burst in like someone who is impatient to tell a story. On seeing the guest, he became confused and seemed almost frightened. But this was momentary and almost immediately his good humor returned.

"Good evening," he said. "A Jew? Welcome. You have been waiting for me, hm?"

"Light the lamp in the other room," the rebbetzin ordered Tsirele.

"Yes, Mama."

Tsirele got up and went into the other room. Max quickly examined her figure. Not tall, but slender, with a narrow waist. He took everything in at a glance: the girlish shoulders, small feet, flat bosom, white neck—delicate as a child's. A nice piece of goods.

"Rabbi, I've come from far-off lands and I heard about you," he said. "I want to contribute toward a good cause."

"Indeed? With pleasure! There are yeshivas, congregations, and just plain folks in Warsaw who need help. Come in. Why sit in the kitchen? Feel welcome." And the rabbi extended a small hand. Max held it awhile in his paw. He towered over the rabbi, looking down upon him as if he were a cheder boy.

The rabbi and Max went into the other room. Tsirele had already lit the hurricane lamp. Max saw walls lined with books and the Holy Ark hung with a ceremonial curtain. At the top, two lions were holding the tablets of the Ten Commandments, their manes embossed in gold leaf. They had red tongues, raised tails, and their glassy eyes shimmered with a kind of holy wildness. Heaped on a lectern near the window were religious books and sheets of paper covered with writing. In the middle of the room stood a table, a chair, and two benches.

What is this? A studyhouse, a synagogue? Max wondered. He had not expected the kitchen to lead into a holy place. He became apprehensive over the lie he had just cooked up—that he was a widower.

Tsirele smiled. "This is our parlor. In America people probably arrange things differently."

"We also have synagogues," said Max, "but the rabbi lives separately."

"It's not a synagogue. On Saturday a congregation prays here," the rabbi said almost apologetically. "The ark is theirs but the religious books are mine."

"Is rent high here?" Max asked.

"Twenty-four rubles a month. We have another room and a balcony. For Warsaw it's not too expensive. On the other streets rents are higher."

"Rabbi, I want to contribute something toward your rent. Fifty rubles."

The rabbi looked at his daughter. "What for? We don't need it. Of course it's hard to pay the rent. But, thank God, we manage."

"Is your daughter engaged?" Max asked, bewildered by his own words.

The rabbi thought for a while as if he himself didn't remember whether his daughter was engaged or not. In Tsirele's glance a mixture of laughter and regret appeared. She turned red, but the redness covered only half her face.

"Do sit," the rabbi said. "It's like this. She is not engaged, but people have been proposing matches. According to custom a daughter brings a dowry to her husband. But an assistant rabbi cannot afford a dowry. Well, for everyone there is a destined match. Where are you from? What do you do?"

Tsirele moved closer to the door but remained there, waiting. Perhaps her father would tell her to bring in tea or refreshments. She threw questioning looks at Max that were both admonishing and silently suggestive.

With this girl I'll be able to come to an understanding, Max concluded. In short order I'll be able to make a date with her.

The rabbi sat down carefully in a chair on which lay a cushion covered with black oilcloth.

"As for where I live, I live in Argentina," Max said, "but I've just been over the whole world—London, New York, Paris, Berlin. My business is selling houses and lots."

"Is that right? What's going on in the world? Jews are Jews, eh?"

"Yes, Rabbi, Jews are Jews. But not like here. In Whitechapel there are synagogues and ritual baths and all of that, but the younger generation speaks English. You talk with one of them and suddenly he will say, 'I am a Jew.' If he hadn't said so, you wouldn't know. In Paris, they speak French. In Argentina, the younger generation has begun to speak Spanish."

"There is a ban on Jews living in Spain," the rabbi said half to himself, half to the guest.

"Argentina is not Spain. The Spaniards came there and conquered the land. They drove out the Indians and killed them."

"What did they do to deserve that?"

"Why did the Jews kill off the people that once lived in the Land of Israel?" Tsirele spoke up suddenly from near the door. "They were also fathers and mothers of children. Why did they deserve to be annihilated?"

The rabbi shivered. He had apparently not realized that his daughter was still there. He tugged at his beard and then immediately let it go. He had taken off his hat and remained in his skullcap. A crease appeared on his high forehead.

"That's what the Almighty decreed. Those people, the seven nations, were entirely sunken in sin. 'There's no end to the abominations in this world.' When an earthen pot becomes ritually impure, it must be broken. That's how it is with cities and nations. When a whole city embarks on idolatry, then it becomes a forbidden city. There comes a time when a person has sunk so deeply into sinfulness that it is no longer possible to repent."

"In what way are the little children responsible?" Tsirele asked. "The little children haven't sinned."

The rabbi grimaced and his voice became hoarse. "Because of the sins of the fathers, the little children must suffer. When fathers and mothers rebel against the Creator and get involved in witchcraft and all manner of unclean things, then no one can be protected."

"That is not right, Father."

"What are you saying? What is it with you? One cannot have more compassion than the Creator. It is written: 'And the souls I created . . .' You'd better bring in the tea." He turned to Max. "Will you perhaps have something with it?"

"Rabbi, I would like to ask your daughter to go out and bring up something. I'll give her money. Just a minute!"

Max went over to the door and handed Tsirele two ten-ruble banknotes. "Please, Fräulein, bring up something, some cookies or fruit. I will eat, too, and honor the good man."

"Twenty rubles for cookies?"

"The rest you can keep for yourself. To study Russian."

Tsirele looked behind her as if she suspected her mother of eavesdropping. She murmured to herself: "An extraordinary man!"

ax had been sleeping for several hours. When he awoke, he saw by the clock that it was not even 3 a.m. Daylight was beginning to show at the windows. He got out of bed and began to exercise, raising his hands, his legs, bending right and left, forward and back.

In his dreams he had not only been enjoying the company of Rochelle but that of his old girlfriends. He dreamed of Tsirele, too, of traveling with her on a ship. He had also taken other women with him, penned up like chickens in coops. As he brought food to them he said, "Doesn't the captain know what's going on, or is he just pretending to be ignorant?" A gale came up and the ship was driven, of all places, to Siberia. Is there an ocean in Siberia, Max wondered, or does this ship fly in the air? How strange! The women he had been talking to were half human, half hens. They were all cackling, and then one began crowing like a rooster. Suddenly Tsirele said, "We'll have to slaughter her." And with that Max gave a start and woke up full of lust.

He wanted to bathe and rang for the chambermaid. But no one came at this early hour. In the hotel where he had stayed in Berlin there had been a bath in his room, but here a bathtub and hot water had to be ordered. He washed at the sink, rubbing his skin with a towel soaked in salt water—a remedy for nerves. He stood where he could look out the window. The street stretched before him, empty, not a droshky, trolley, or passerby in sight. Dew had fallen on the trees and the birds were twittering. Max returned to his bed.

Once again he began to dream. This time he found himself in a city that was both Buenos Aires and New York. His ship, after riding out a storm, had arrived at port and the passengers were being taken to Ellis Island. Rochelle had disguised herself as a man, but from under her jacket a pair of women's bloomers protruded. Even a blind man could see what she had done. Max screamed at her to hide the lace, but she didn't listen to him. He struck her with his fist and awoke covered with sweat, his heart palpitating. "I'll go crazy from all these dreams!" Max said to himself. He now felt weak, while in his dreams he had been his old vigorous self.

Again he had to douse himself with cold water to quell his desire. It seemed to him that he had slept only a few minutes, but the clock said ten to six. In the street a few trolleys were clanging, and janitors were sweeping the pavement with brooms, spraying water from hoses.

By the time he got dressed it was seven. He walked a few blocks until he came to a coffeehouse, ready to go in and order breakfast, when he remembered Haym Kaviornik, the man who had said that he had the best cheese buns in the world. I'll just ride over there, Max decided, and he quickly found a droshky. When the coachman heard that he wanted to go to Krochmalna

Street, he turned up his nose. But still, he waved his whip. "Giddyap!"

Max leaned against the side of the coach. Who knows? Perhaps he would see her. The rabbi had mentioned a balcony. Would Tsirele come out on the balcony? Max closed his eyes. This is crazy, he mused. I'll get myself in so deep that seven pairs of oxen won't be able to pull me out. Well, he had experienced too many failures and he must break the spell. Something must happen, he told himself. Rochelle could become seriously ill; she might even agree to a divorce if he parted with half his wealth. The main thing was not to remain passive.

The droshky passed through many streets whose names he did not know. Soon they reached a Jewish neighborhood and Max recognized the façade of the Vienna Hall. Below, between the building's pillars, vendors were selling tablecloths, towels, linen, thread, buttons, remnants. The air was permeated with the fragrance of cherries, strawberries, currants, and other summer smells. Max breathed in deeply, inhaling an odor of horse manure. Even Krochmalna Street appeared fresher than yesterday. The square was not so heavily populated.

The droshky stopped at No. 8 and Max gave the coachman a forty-groschen piece. He caught sight of the coffeehouse, went inside, and recognized Haym Kaviornik. He was now wearing a long apron and the white hat of a cook, and he called out: "As I live and breathe, the American!" Clapping his hands, he pointed to a chair. "Sit yourself down. You won't go hungry here."

"The smell of your cheese buns fills the street."

"They come here for my buns from as far away as Muranow. May we both live and be well."

"Would you perhaps have a Jewish newspaper?"

Haym opened the door, called to a vendor, and immediately a girl brought in a Jewish paper. Never had Max been so hungry for Jewish words. The political news on the front page seemed to him the same as yesterday's. But the local news was full of disasters—a flood in Lublin, a strike of railroad workers in Russia, a fire in Warsaw fatal to many victims. Under the headline A MAN, AN ANIMAL Max read: "Late last night, Yan Lopata, a watchman at 12 Smocza Street, came home drunk and threw himself on his daughter, Marianna, eleven years old. The mother tried to prevent the drunkard's brutal attack, but he stabbed her with his knife. After that he raped his own child. On hearing the screams of neighbors, the police came and arrested the bestial father and led him away in chains. His wife is in the Holy Ghost Hospital in critical condition."

Max ate his cheese bun, trying to imagine the meaning of what he had read. As sweet as this cheese bun's taste is, that's how bitter life can be, he thought. Who knows what mad ideas can possess a father? He, Max, had never had a daughter, but hadn't people in ancient times done similar things? Didn't Jacob marry two sisters? In Argentina, Peru, Bolivia, Chile, and elsewhere daughters are raped by fathers, brothers couple with sisters, a mother has relations with her own son. People don't always get arrested for such crimes; they go to the priest to confess and he absolves them with woe water. The Indians lived according to one-thousand-year-old customs . . . Well, Yan Lopata is no doubt serving time on a plank bed in the Powiak prison.

"Another glass of coffee?" Haym Kaviornik brought the hot brew himself and sat down on a chair across from Max. "What does the newspaper say?"

"Many disasters."

"Do you think they write an honest word? Those writers sometimes make up lies. Where you lived abroad, did people know what was going on here?"

"We have newspapers there, too."

"Did you hear about the Japanese war?"

"Yes, everything."

"Here the riots got hot and heavy and I had to close the coffeehouse. The strikers said everyone should be equal, and there should not be a Tsar. When I asked if I should overthrow the Tsar, they retorted, 'You, too, are a bourgeois, you suck our blood.' That's how they talked to me. Someone had to read— what do you call it?—a proclamation to them. They can't read. When they find such papers on anyone, he is sent to Siberia. When the news came out that the Tsar was giving in, they marched to the town hall and were greeted with bullets. They fell like flies. The Cossacks rode in on their horses and slashed heads with their sabers. The punks on the street, the thieves, the fences, the pimps got into it, and it became a real battle. The strikers then jumped in and beat up the whores—a madam was beaten violently. There's a man around here called Blind Mayer who was stabbed five times."

"Blind Mayer? Where is he?"

"Do you know him?"

"I've heard the name."

"He was the leader of the hoodlums. Rabbi, that's what they called him. When a person was robbed, he went to Blind Mayer and paid him ransom money, and when Blind Mayer ordered the thief to give the loot back, everything was returned down to the last groschen. Today he's no longer the big boss. He's blind in one eye and the other can hardly see. A new generation has come up; as it says in the Pentateuch, 'And he did not know Joseph.' You know what that means, ha?"

"I studied a bit in cheder."

"These things get lost, but something remains. I wake up in the middle of the night remembering a verse in Scripture, and later I forget again. I heard that you went to the rabbi yesterday and gave him a few rubles."

Max Barabander pushed his glass away. "Who told you?"

"People know everything around here. The rabbi is a good man, a pauper to the nth degree. He had a son who became a modern Jew and left home. He put on a hat with a cape and his father sat in mourning for him. You met Tsirele, eh?"

"Yes, she was there."

"A good girl, but her father has no pleasure from her. Too modern. They talked to her about marrying the son of a cheder teacher, Reb Zaynvele, but she didn't want the match. When her mother persisted, she tried to jump off the balcony. I was there and heard her scream. She ran out dressed only in a chemise and tried to leap over the railing. Suicide, that's what it's called. The rabbi himself ran after her without a coat, in his ritual undergarment, and the skullcap fell off his head. The match came to naught. She comes here every morning to buy the gazette. You're a widower, right?"

"Yes, a widower."

"What kind of racket is going on outside? I'll take a look."

When Haym went outside, Max took a swallow of coffee. It had already paid to come here. Besides a delicious breakfast, he had learned something about Tsirele. If a girl is capable of such rage, you have to watch out. On the other hand, such a girl is hot-blooded. Perhaps she could be easily seduced.

Haym came back in. "A glazier fell from a window on the third floor."

"Did he get killed?"

"Broke a leg."

Max thought, He is luckier than me. They'll take him to the hospital and fix his leg. Max called the waiter, paid, and nodded goodbye to Haym.

On leaving the coffeehouse he caught a glimpse of the balcony outside the rabbi's rooms. A young boy with red side-locks was standing there in an unbuttoned robe, from which his fringed undergarment protruded. The balcony was so low that Max felt he could almost touch it. He called out: "Hey, what's your name?"

"Me? Itchele."

"Your father's the rabbi?"

"Yes."

"Is he at home?"

"No."

"And your mother?"

"She's not here."

"Who's at home?"

"My sister."

Something tore at Max's insides. "I'll go up. What can happen? If she throws me out, the world won't come to an end." He went in at the gate. "Have I fallen in love with her?" he asked himself. "No, this isn't love but stubbornness, the desire to break down a wall." He had come to Poland to perpetrate he knew not what. If he couldn't get himself out of the hole, he had nothing to go back home for. He was like a roulette player who puts his entire fortune on the spinning wheel.

When Max knocked on the door, no one answered. He turned the knob, the door opened, and he saw Tsirele. She was sitting on an iron bedstead reading a Yiddish newspaper. In the light of the sun, he could really appreciate her beauty. She was the kind of brunette whose hair shades into golden blond. Her face and neck were dazzling white. Her cheeks showed two red spots, sometimes seen in people with consumption and also in young girls who have just outgrown their childhood. Tsirele looked younger than the night before. When she spotted Max, her blue eyes smiled for a moment with a radiant joy peculiar to the female sex. But she quickly became serious and took a hesitant step backward. Over her dress she wore a black faille pinafore, like a student.

"Don't be afraid, Tsirele," said Max. "I won't harm you. I went to the coffeehouse here at No. 8 to—what's his name —Haym Kaviornik and I noticed your brother on the balcony. He and you are alike as two drops of water."

Tsirele laid the newspaper down. "He didn't go to cheder today because it's a *galuevka*."

"What's that?"

"It's the Tsar's uncle's birthday. Itchele goes to a government cheder and there all the Christian holidays are celebrated."

Max had not completely absorbed what she said, but her voice intoxicated him. It had the same hoarseness as that good man, her father, but it also rang like a bell. Her lips parted, revealing milk-white teeth. "She's charming," Max said to himself. He had an urge to fly to her, take her in his arms, and crush her against him with all his might, to carry her off someplace where he could be alone with her, to get drunk on her flesh. But at the same time he knew he must keep himself in check. She's the daughter of a rabbi and her brother is at home.

"I want to talk to you about something which is only for your own good," he said.

"Oh? My mother is not at home. I have to prepare dinner soon."

"Perhaps you would like to have dinner with me? I'll take you to—what do you call it?—a restaurant. I want to talk to you."

"What do you want to talk to me about? That's all I need—to go out in the street with you. It's like a small town here, even worse. Everybody knows what's cooking in their neighbor's pot. My mother—" And Tsirele broke off. She looked at him wryly, curious, half afraid. She said, "I still have the change from the money you gave me yesterday." She made a motion as if to take the money out of her stocking.

Max looked at her in surprise. "I don't want your money. Just the opposite; I want to give you more. Perhaps we can meet somewhere outside. What's the garden called where Jews are not allowed?"

"The Saxony Gardens? Jews are allowed, but only those that are not in long clothes, and a woman has to wear a hat."

"I'll buy you a hat."

Tsirele looked at him with bewilderment and suspicion. "What would people say? The rabbi's daughter! They would drive my father out of Warsaw."

Max moved a step closer. "Your father isn't known in all of Warsaw. Perhaps only on this street. Go out on Marszalkowska Boulevard and no one will know who you are. We'll go into a shop and buy you the prettiest hat in Warsaw. Then we'll get into a droshky and go—"

"Go? Where?" Tsirele asked in the eager voice of a child who has been promised grownup pleasures.

"Oh, to the garden or far away to New World Street. I can't remember what the avenue is called."

"Jerusalem Avenue. I can't go, because I have to get dinner ready. My mother went to No. 12 to see an old friend there, a woman. We eat dinner at two o'clock; my little brother Moishe returns from cheder and—"

"Let's meet after dinner."

"Where? If I go someplace I must say where. Mama is nervous. She starts to worry and gets palpitations. If I go out for an hour, I have to give an account of every move."

"On such a beautiful day everyone goes for a walk, even a rabbi's daughter. Come over to the Hotel Bristol, where I'll wait for you. We'll take a droshky and nobody will recognize us. You could even be my daughter. I'll buy you a hat, shoes, whatever you need. We'll be together for a while and later you'll go back in a droshky. Maybe you want to go to the theater or to the opera. I'll buy seats in the first row."

Tsirele licked her upper lip. "You don't get home from the theater until twelve o'clock at night. They would think I was kidnapped or something. My mother would die of fright. My father—"

"We don't have to go to the theater. We could go to a café, take a ride over the Praga bridge. When I heard you talking yesterday, I realized that you are no fool. You understand what life is all about, but your parents are—fanatics. They will marry you off to a *shmagegy* and shave your head. They'll put a wig made of silk hair on your head and you'll have a house full of filthy children."

Tsirele looked serious. "Yes, it's true, but—"

"Why but? Come to the Hotel Bristol after dinner. If you are afraid to come upstairs, I'll wait for you outside. I'm not poor, I have money. My wife is dead and I have, as they say, neither kith nor kin. I want to be good but I need someone to be good to," said Max, enchanted by his own words.

He himself didn't know whether he was trying to lead the girl, the rabbi's daughter, astray or whether he wanted to share his life with her. A great doctor in Berlin, a psychiatrist who knew Yiddish, had told Max that the best cure for his condition was to fall in love. With Tsirele I would become a man again, Max thought, not sure if he was really convinced or was trying to persuade himself of this.

Tsirele hesitatingly laid the newspaper on the bed. "I'm afraid someone would recognize us."

"Nobody will see you."

"What will I do with the hat when I get home? They will ask me how I got it."

"Ha? I'll talk to your parents. I'll tell them I want to marry you." It was as if a dybbuk had spoken within him.

Tsirele took a quick look at the door. "Oh, how you talk!"

"I'm almost thirty years older than you," he said, suddenly addressing her with the familiar *thou*, "but I am not an old man. We could take a trip together around the world. I will get a teacher for you, not just any old teacher who charges twenty kopecks, but a professor who would teach you Russian, German, French, whatever you want. I want to study, too. What's the saying? 'Better late than never.' I have money enough, thank God. We would go to Paris, London, New York. You're no country bumpkin. I took one look at you and knew right away how fine you are."

The color in Tsirele's face changed with strange rapidity.

Terror registered in her eyes as well as the confusion of someone who urgently needs to speak but holds back. First she redid her braid with her right hand, then the left. Her hands were small and white just like her father's. "Please, someone could come by and overhear us," she burst out.

"What time will you come?" asked Max, sure that she would come.

Tsirele's eyes were full of inquiry. "Four o'clock?"

"Yes, four o'clock."

"At the Hotel Bristol?"

"Yes, there."

"Perhaps across the street?"

"Let it be across the street."

"I'll come, but . . . I'll have to walk home. A droshky is no good. People talk behind my back as it is—you'll never know how much . . . They tried to force me . . . against my nature . . . Better to die . . . quite simply . . ."

"Yes, I understand."

"Someone told you?"

"Yes, when I was eating breakfast at Haym Kaviornik's."

"Oh, don't tell anyone. If someone should find out, there would be such talk."

"Whom will I tell? I don't know anyone here. If you want, I'll talk to your parents."

"They would never—" Tsirele broke off.

"You never know. They don't have a dowry for you. All those yeshiva boys have to get room and board from the bride's side and whatever goes with it. Was there a pogrom here?"

"No, but people were shot . . . In this very court there was a boy called Vova, whose mother was a widow. He went to a demonstration and was never seen alive again."

"Were you in love with him?"

"No, but—"

"Well, I'll go now. Remember, four o'clock across from the Hotel Bristol."

"Yes, four o'clock."

Max was about to say goodbye when the door to the prayer room was flung open and the boy with red sidelocks ran in. Seeing Max, he stepped back. "Oh, you're the one who talked to me on the balcony!" he said, pointing at Max.

Max took a good look at him. Having been out of the country for so many years, he had forgotten how Jewish children dressed in Poland. The boy was wearing a crumpled, fuzzy little velvet hat with a visor on the side. His face, as white as his sister's, was smeared. On his little smock the only remaining button dangled. His boots were patched and his toes stuck out. His ritual undergarment hung askew, with one tassel higher than the other. Max sized him up with an experienced eye. The lad was embarrassed and had hurriedly stuffed his shirt into his pants.

Tsirele started up and scolded him. "Just take a look at yourself . . . We put a fresh shirt on him, but right away it gets black as the earth," she explained to Max. "He rolls around in the muck."

"Well, it doesn't matter. A child is a child," Max excused him. "What did you say your name is?"

"Itchele."

"Do you go to cheder?"

"Not today."

"What are you studying, Pentateuch?"

"Pentateuch, Commentaries, Talmud."

"What's the passage today?"

"*Shlakh.*"

Max fell silent. He had once studied Scripture but had forgotten everything. The word *shlakh* had stirred something in him. I must ride over to Roszkow, he reminded himself.

"Here's a forty-groschen piece," he said to Itchele, who stretched out his hand. Tsirele wrinkled her brows.

"Don't give it to him! What does he need money for? He'll just buy sweets and get worms in his belly."

"I *won't* get worms."

"Here, take it," said Max. "Buy what you want and don't tell your mother. You won't tell, right?"

"No."

"Don't tell her that anyone was here. Go and buy what you want. My name is Max."

"Max? That's not a Jewish name."

"My real name is Mordkhe, but in America Mordkhe becomes Max."

"You live in America?"

"What's this familiar *thou?*" Tsirele said angrily. "To an older person you use the polite form."

"I forgot."

"It doesn't matter. He can say *thou* to me. You, too, Tsirele. As soon as I came to your house yesterday I felt at home, as if I had come back to my parents—may they rest in Paradise. I went to cheder and all the rest. I had a rabbi who was called Shepsl Banak, at least that was his nickname. In Roszkow everyone has a nickname: Berele Buck, Fayvele Scratch Me, Hershele Pudding-Head. One man was called Zaynvele Kishke-Eater. What will you buy with the money, eh?" he asked the boy.

"I won't buy any candy."

"No? What, then?"

"A Talmud. I read from the same Talmud with another boy. But he pulls the Talmud over to his side and doesn't let me see. Later, when it's time to be examined, I don't know the passage and the rabbi starts to yell."

"A Talmud costs only twenty kopecks?"

"A little Talmud."

"Here's another forty-groschen piece to buy yourself a nosh. You'll buy one little Talmud and you'll still have something left for a fling. But don't tell anyone that I was here. Is that a promise?"

"Yes, I won't tell."

"Now I must go!" Max went outside and bumped into a woman. It was not the rebbetzin but someone carrying a chicken; she looked like a market woman.

"There's a reason for me to live again," Max said to himself. He no longer felt the emptiness that had tortured him since Arturo's tragic death. At the gate he turned left. "What will come of all this? Rochelle is alive. I'm not a widower . . ." He headed slowly in the direction of Gnoyna Street.

"A drowning man grasps at a straw," he said aloud to himself.

That evening it rained and the coachman had to put up the carriage hood. Max embraced Tsirele and kissed her. He felt her trembling like a little bird. Choking, she pushed him away. Her face became extraordinarily flushed. It had been so long since he was seized by desire for a woman, clear and strong as when he was a young man.

"I love you, love you!" he said to her. "We'll get married. You will be the mother of my children! . . ." Tsirele's heart was beating so fast that Max became frightened. I'll divorce Rochelle, he decided. I'll take Tsirele to Africa, to the ends of the earth!

The droshky had arrived at Gnoyna Street and Max ordered the driver to stop, since Tsirele did not want to arrive home in the droshky. Max had promised to get her home by nine o'clock and it was already a quarter to ten. The rain stopped and the wet bridge glistened, its stones reflecting the lights of the gas lamps. A cool breeze blew in from the river.

Max gave Tsirele a parting kiss, paid the coachman, and helped Tsirele climb out. "I'll be at your house tomorrow morning," he said. "I'll speak openly with your parents."

"Oh, I'm afraid! What shall I say to them? They're probably looking for me already."

"Say whatever you want. You can even tell them that you were with me. We'll get married anyway."

"They might not want that—you don't have a beard."

"Better a Jew without a beard than a beard without a Jew," said Max, citing a couplet from the Yiddish theater. "If they don't agree, then we'll run away."

He stood and watched her turn into Krochmalna Street. She looked back and threw him a glance full of fear and love. No, he had not taken this trip in vain. He was a man again. A young girl was in love with him and was ready to become his wife—a pure virgin, the rabbi's daughter. From between the clouds a sliver of moon appeared and Max breathed deeply. Well, the crisis was over. Did it mean there is a God who watches over each and every one of us?

For one moment Max thought he would return to the hotel, but no, it was too early for him to go to sleep. He remembered the baker woman, Esther, and her invitation. It was a perfect time. He began striding with long steps and thought, From now on everything will go my way.

When he came to No. 15, he caught a glimpse of the rabbi's window on the first floor. It was lighted. Tsirele was surely at home by now. He put two fingers to his lips and in his thoughts sent her a kiss. She is exactly what I need: young, pretty, not too wily, not fanatical. The rabbi will consent: when your daughter tries to jump off a balcony, you can't expect her to make a great match.

As Max passed by the gate he became aware of bakery smells: caraway and poppy seeds, fresh bagels, sour dough. In a cellar, down some steps, a baker was placing bread in the oven with a paddle. In the middle of the room stood a vat of boiling water, and a man clad only in his underwear, barefoot, with a conical paper hat on his head, was throwing raw bagels into it. At a giant trough stretching from wall to wall, half-naked youths were kneading dough, yelling to each other and laughing. It put Max in mind of stories about hell he had heard in his youth, where people kindled the fires in which they themselves would burn for their sins.

A man whitened with flour, carrying a board covered with loaves of raw dough, came by. "Where does the baker live?" Max asked.

"Right there on the second floor."

Max started up the darkened stairs lit by a tiny kerosene lamp in a black and sooty glass. He didn't have to knock, the door stood open. He heard talking, laughter, a clattering of dishes. Three women were sitting at a table eating a late-night meal. They were so engrossed that they did not hear Max's footsteps. He stood awhile in the doorway and watched them.

He not only recognized Esther but decided who was her sister and who was her daughter. When Max gave a little cough, the three women looked up. Esther placed her glass on the saucer.

"Mamelekh, he's here!" Rising quickly, she exclaimed, "I had given up on you!" And she clapped her hands.

In a moment Max was sitting at the table. They had already been talking about him. The whole street knew about his visit to the rabbi. Tsirele was right: Krochmalna Street was like a small town. Max had already eaten an evening meal, but he immediately felt hungry again and Esther went off to the kitchen.

Esther's sister looked like her except that she was fairer, with a higher bosom and broader shoulders. The sister wore her hair swept up, with a braid on top, like a Rosh Hashanah challah. Shmuel Smetena had called Esther's younger sister a beauty, but Max preferred the older one.

The daughter evidently took after her father—tall, heavy, blond, the type Krochmalna Street would call a hefty broad. Her laugh was loud and ringing. She chewed with both cheeks full. In no time she would have a double chin, and in a few years would spread out like a piece of rising dough.

Esther brought in a tray with a bottle of brandy and some small glasses.

"We're not drunks," she said, "but in honor of our guest we'll take a sip of brandy."

When the talk moved on to the rabbi and Shmuel Smetena, Esther said, "Shmuel is capable of the worst, but he likes to do favors. If there is money to be had, he wants to be paid well but he will take care of a poor man free of charge. The rabbi missed going to the police station by a hair."

"Does Shmuel have a wife and children?"

"He has a wife and children but only on the Sabbath," Esther's sister, Celia, piped up. "The whole week he's never seen at home."

"He goes around with other women?"

"One woman and a good one."

"We should all earn every day what he loses every week in cards," Esther interjected. "Around here they play cards in a watchman's hut at No. 11. Many a foolish Hasid has lost his dowry there."

"What do people play?"

"Oke, Bank, Sixty-six, Thousand, whatever you can think of. Once someone used marked cards and took everybody, but he left with broken bones in an ambulance."

"The police don't interfere?"

"They get a part of every stake . . ."

Max took a glass of brandy and felt cheerful. He ate an onion roll and it had the taste he remembered. After a while Celia began to yawn. Esther's daughter, Dasha, said that her husband was waiting for her.

Max got up. "Well, it's time for me to go, too."

"What's your hurry?" Esther asked. "Unless there's some-one waiting for you at the Hotel Bristol."

"Who—the Queen of Sheba?"

"Then stay. I never go to sleep before two."

When the others left, Esther's face became older and sterner.

"Where is your husband?" Max asked.

"In Lazar's bar."

"Who takes care of the bakery?"

"Nobody. It could have been a gold mine. It's a miracle we make a living." Esther played with her fork, and wrinkled her brow. "Peysakh was the best baker in Warsaw. When I became his fiancée, everyone said I had fallen into a pot of gold. He could have driven out all the other bakers in the neighborhood. But a few years after we got married he started drinking. The helpers do whatever they want. He's rid himself of every responsibility: his daughter, the bakery, the house. Either he is drinking or he lies on the sacks in the bakery and snores. He shames me in front of other people and doesn't keep the holidays or the Sabbath. Do you have a wife and children?" Esther asked.

"Had."

"What happened?"

"Taken by the Angel of Death."

"You are still young."

"Troubles make you old." He had an impulse to talk about Tsirele but stopped himself. He lit a cigarette, blew smoke rings. "What's the use of money if you have no one to share it with? Even Rothschild eats only one dinner a day. The Riviera is so beautiful, but sitting alone in a railroad car you get tired of looking at it."

"You can't find a woman you would desire?"

"The young ones are too young and those that are my age have husbands."

"I should have a thousand rubles for every widow in Warsaw."

"If you take a widow then you sleep with her husband," said Max, not sure whether this was his own thought or he had read it somewhere.

He rose and began to pace up and down. Esther also got up from the table. He knew that if he loved Tsirele, he mustn't get involved with this baker lady, a grandmother with a grandchild. But, as the saying goes, even before you reach a good tavern, you could use a nip. He went over to Esther, put his arms around her waist, and embraced her. She made no move to pull away. Her knees rested against his and he kissed her on the lips. She asked, "So soon?"

"At our age you can't wait too long."

"Just a moment, I'll bolt the door."

The moment Esther said these words, Max felt his desire wane. The same thing had happened many times before. As soon as the woman consented, something inside him began to cool off, shrink, and he was overcome by shame and anxiety. A little brandy was left and he quickly downed it. The alcohol went straight to his head, but the fear did not evaporate.

Esther lingered a lot longer than it takes to bolt a door. Perhaps she was washing herself, changing her clothes. He looked at the window as if ready to jump out. He thought, I want someone only when they are not willing.

Five minutes passed; then Esther suddenly put her head through the door. She had undressed and put on a bathrobe. She made a motion for him to follow her to the bedroom. He waved his hand to say that he would follow. On tiptoe he went to the outside door, struggled with the lock, and stepped out.

Max ran in the direction of Ciepla Street. The evening's victory had ended in bitter defeat. "God in heaven. This is the end!"

Max Barabander undressed and lay on his bed, knowing beforehand that he wouldn't sleep a wink. The windows were open but there wasn't even a hint of a breeze. Max lay motionless. His neck, shoulders, and legs felt itchy, but he didn't scratch. When a man his age can no longer take pleasure in a woman, then eating, drinking, dressing, traveling around the world, everything becomes a burden.

"There is only one way out," Max said to himself. "Suicide." But how would he do it? Shoot himself, jump out the window, drown himself in the Vistula, take poison, hang himself? Max had noticed a hook on the ceiling, but he realized he was not ready to find a rope, make a noose, and place a stool under it. In the same way that his madness began, it could also end. Death can never come too late. And then what if there is a God? Demons? Paradise? Hell? Perhaps the day after his death he would have to stand before God's throne . . .

Lying stretched out in bed, unable to move, Max took stock of his life. His father had been a pious man, a coachman, who had given away his last coin so that he, Max—Motl as he was called—could go to cheder. But he was never drawn to learning. He skimped on saying his prayers, played a game of buttons on the Sabbath, and hung on to the backs of wagons. Early on, he was drawn to girls and to getting into fights with Gentile and Jewish boys. He had acquired a reputation in Roszkow for being a joker, a prankster, a bit of an ass. At the age of fifteen, he went off with a Gentile girl, Wanda, who cleaned out barns. He stole from Jews and peasants. His father apprenticed him to a tailor, but he had no patience for tailoring. At the first chance he got, he fled to Warsaw.

But he hadn't remained entirely ignorant. His education came from reading chapbooks, Jewish newspapers, and even books. He had read Shomer, Isaac Meir Dick, all kinds of almanacs, and even such writers as Linetzki, Mendele Mocher Sforim, Sholem Aleichem, Hermalin, and Seifert. He remembered innumerable jokes and anecdotes that he had heard from traveling salesmen, thieves, fences, and shop clerks. He had become expert in seducing women and young girls. He had never learned to write a letter without mistakes, but he had a glib tongue in Yiddish, Polish, and Russian. He loved the opera, theater, circus, and ballet.

God in heaven! He had made conquests that he could never even boast of, because people would take him for a liar. His sweethearts were chorus girls, cabaret dancers, even an actress who played leading roles at the Muranow Theater. For a time in Argentina he had got close to the owners of houses of prostitution. Indeed, it was in these surroundings that he met Rochelle. However, he had vowed not to stay stuck in the mire.

As soon as Max got some money together, he made business trips all over South America, North America and Canada. He understood what the Zionists and socialists wanted. He became acquainted with anarchists, vegetarians, with those who preached that Jews should settle in Baron de Hirsch's colonies, and even with the Tolstoyans, who tilled the soil and lived according to Tolstoy's tenets. He subscribed to a Jewish newspaper and journal from New York and in time became friends with New York actors and actresses who came on tour to Buenos Aires.

Yet he never lost his underworld mentality. He had fantasies about great robberies, counterfeiting rings, and get-rich-quick schemes. After he had broken with his disreputable friends and became a member of the Burial Society, which admitted only the most respectable community members, he still couldn't stop dreaming of shady deals. Nor could he rid himself of the desire to corrupt innocent women, to entice a wife away from her husband, a fiancée away from her betrothed. In his fantasies he still carried girls off on ships to Buenos Aires and other

South American countries. When Rochelle was pregnant, Max trembled for fear she might give birth to a girl.

Although Max was not an intellectual, he had his own philosophy. In what way were the so-called honest people better than the prostitutes, thieves, and pimps? The merchants swindled, the housewives cheated on their husbands. Weren't there books and plays about prostitutes and murderers? At least the underworld didn't pretend that it was holy. According to his lights, Max had complaints against God. The world didn't create itself, someone must be in charge of this little planet, but who is he? What does he want? Nobody was there when God gave Moses the Ten Commandments. You'd better take what you can get. But what could he take?

At daybreak, Max fell fast asleep, and an hour and a half later he woke up. At eight o'clock Max rang for the chambermaid and she readied a bath for him. In the bathroom he took off his robe and examined his body in the mirror. He had gained some weight but his muscles were still hard, his vital juices still flowed, and his old powers lay in wait. He was but a step away from his old strength. Something had stuck fast in his soul. Sorrow, regret, and shame possessed him like a dybbuk. It occurred to Max that yes, perhaps he should go and see a rabbi, perhaps that good man Tsirele's father. "But no, I can't confide in him about such things."

When Max sat down to breakfast, he leafed through the newspaper and after a while started scanning the personal ads. One caught his eye: "Famous clairvoyant Bernard Shkolnikov predicts your future by reading your palm and forehead, locates missing persons and objects, uncovers thieveries, shows you your loved ones in a mirror. Reasonable prices. Receives visitors from ten in the morning until eight in the evening." The address and telephone number followed. Max stopped chewing for a while. Maybe this man could help him. Perhaps the higher power that watches over the world didn't let him throw that newspaper into the wastebasket. I'll get to the clairvoyant today, Max decided.

Who knows? There are hidden secrets that one cannot fathom. A gypsy had once foretold certain things about him that proved to be true in every respect. And how? With a pack of soiled cards. There is magic; yes, there is. Perhaps someone had put a curse on him or cast the Evil Eye. Rochelle herself was something of a witch . . . Max had begun eating with little desire for food, but this advertisement had whetted his appetite. He carefully cut out the ad and put it in his vest pocket.

Just as Max was ready to leave the room, there was a knock at the door and a bellboy in a red uniform with gilded buttons and a round hat said, "Mr. Barabander? You are wanted on the telephone."

"On the telephone?"

It's always like that. The moment you begin to feel a ray of hope, something comes up. But who could be telephoning him? Who knew he was staying at the Hotel Bristol? The telephone was in the corridor. Max picked up the receiver.

"Who is calling?"

"Is this Max Barabander?" said a man with an oily voice, the sound coming not from his chest but as if wrested from his bowels.

"Yes, that's me," Max answered.

"This is Shmuel Smetena. We met the day before yesterday in the tavern at No. 17. Do you remember?"

"What a question! Of course I remember."

"Good! I like that. I hate people who are stuck up. The

minute I took a look at you, I knew you were one of us. Last night we went to the tavern again and everybody asked for you. Esther, too, the woman from the bakery at No. 15. You're lucky with women."

"I used to be."

"There's an old Polish saying: 'Where there was water, there will be water.' Why don't you come over again? It's like this, I want to talk something over with you, but not in the tavern. I have a friend, a wonderful woman. We're like family. I don't keep any secrets from her. She lives at No. 23 and her cooking is fit for a king. Maybe you could come and eat supper with us, just the three of us."

"What's her name? And what's her apartment number?"

"Eh? Her name is Reyzl. Reyzl Kork. That's how she's known in the neighborhood. The apartment number is 12. The entrance is through the gate, and the apartment is on the second floor. Right after No. 17, you'll find No. 21, and next comes No. 23."

"What time should I come?"

"Around five o'clock. Reyzl wants to know what you like to eat. I love her meatballs, which she makes with egg barley, and prunes and apricots for dessert."

"What could be better than meatballs with egg barley?"

"If you are taking a droshky, tell the driver to come by way of Ciepla Street. Why does everyone on the street have to know where you're going? I'm one who believes in keeping things mum."

"*Bueno*, we'll see each other at five." Only after he hung up did Max remember that *bueno* wasn't Yiddish. That's not how people talked in Poland.

The clairvoyant Bernard Shkolnikov lived on Dluga Street. The droshky drove the length of Cracow Suburbs Street, passed Kozia Street, went into Miodowa Street, and from there to Dluga Street. The house was not far from Krasinski Square. Max Barabander caught a glimpse of the castle. He remembered this neighborhood where he used to go walking with girls. He went into an old house with a narrow entrance and crooked steps, the kind one sees in the old city.

On the third floor it was black as night. He lit a match and read on the door: BERNARD SHKOLNIKOV. He knocked but it was a long time before anyone answered. At last a little man with a tiny black beard and a mustache appeared, wearing what seemed to be a wig. He was dressed in a non-Jewish-looking gabardine coat, striped pants, and slippers. Max observed that he looked sick, worried, frightened.

"I'm the one who telephoned you earlier—Max Barabander."

"I know, come in," he answered in a voice that was both piercing and hoarse.

Max passed through a narrow corridor with walls covered in dark wallpaper. There was a metal lantern hanging from the ceiling. Soon he entered a room where the windows were shrouded in heavy drapes. Pictures of monsters, snakes, skeletons hung on the wall. The chairs were upholstered in black cloth. "All this is done to instill fear," he said to himself. The coldness of a cellar had settled in the room.

Shkolnikov showed Max to a chair and sat down opposite him at a small table. "Where did you say you were from?"

"From Argentina, but I have already lived in half a dozen countries."

"What brings you here?"

Max Barabander began to speak. He told the man about Arturo's death, Rochelle's despair, and how, after a time, he had himself fallen into a depression. Shkolnikov did not interrupt him. He grimaced as if he had a pain in his innards. He drummed on the table with his narrow fingers, which had long, pointed nails, like those of a woman.

Max wasn't sure how long he had been speaking. From time to time, Shkolnikov closed his eyes as if he had fallen asleep. Then he opened them again. He had heavy black eyebrows and a penetrating glance.

"I can't be with a woman, plain and simple," Max blurted out, and fell silent.

Shkolnikov looked up at the window as if he suspected someone was looking in. Does he live here by himself? Max wondered. Or does he have a family?

Shkolnikov scratched his wig. "What do the doctors say?"

"Nerves."

"Nerves," Shkolnikov repeated as if the word itself filled him with disgust. He shuddered, closed one eye, and seemed completely absorbed in thoughts too difficult to express. "Where did they send you? To Carlsbad or to Marienbad?"

"I was everywhere."

"And nothing helped?"

"No."

"You don't need baths," said Shkolnikov, looking off to the corner of the room. "The desire of a male for a female comes from the spirit, not the body. That desire is called potency, a kind of magnetism. Just as a magnet attracts iron, so does a woman attract a man. Not all women have that magnetic power. One woman can be beautiful and leave you cold. Another can be ugly but when you see her she awakens a magnetic power in you. When a man is young that magnetic power is so strong that every woman arouses him. Awhile ago there was a story in the newspaper about a young Gentile boy who raped a seventy-two-year-old woman. When you are older, you must love the woman and she must love you—that's essential. Your wife has stopped loving you, but nevertheless she doesn't want anyone else to have you. If she has strong powers, she can hypnotize you from afar. She can control you through telepathic messages and you don't even know you are being controlled. Just as some-one with greater physical strength can defeat a weaker person, so can someone with greater spiritual power do what they will with a weaker person. You are the weaker one, that's all."

"If so, then there's nothing to be done."

"Yes, there is, there is. Do you perhaps have a photograph of your wife?"

"What? Yes."

"Show me the photograph. The fact that you are here, thousands of miles away, is not significant. The spirit does not recognize distance. You can go to the ends of the earth but her magnetism will still follow you. Show it to me!"

Max handed over the photograph. Bernard Shkolnikov looked at it, grimaced, bit his lips. He turned the photograph over from one side to the other. He began to shake his head as if at an obvious truth.

"Long ago it was called magic," he said. "Now it's called hypnotism. It's all a matter of will. How was Napoleon able to send millions of soldiers off to war? Because his will was stronger than theirs. He lost the war not because the English and Prussian cannons fired better but because his will weakened. When you see a battle going on for a hill or a tower, it may seem that bodies are fighting, but in truth it is a struggle between spirits. Do you understand me?"

"Very well."

"Your wife is simply carrying on a war with you. She wants you to become her absolute slave or simply to surrender. You must oppose her."

"How?"

"That's what I will teach you. You will have to send back messages to her. We have ways of strengthening your magnetism. As you become stronger, she will automatically become weaker. That's exactly what happened with Jacob and Esau. Did you ever go to cheder? 'One rose and the other fell.' And that's not all. The spirits of the dead are also a part of our lives. You had parents, friends, and loved ones who have departed from this world. It may seem to you that they have gone forever. However, they are here and they are eager to help you. You just have to know how to get in contact with them. In the evening I hold séances and we call up the spirits of our dear ones. You needn't be afraid. Spirits cannot harm you. Your parents do not love you any less now than when you were a child."

Max Barabander's emotions choked him. It was hard for him to hold back his tears.

"I never wrote to my parents. I didn't even put up a gravestone for them."

"They have forgiven you. Just as we need to breathe air, they need to breathe love. I cannot predict anything, but you will see for yourself. We hold our séances in the evening and it would be useful for you to come at least twice a week. The main thing is not to doubt and to have patience. I myself am not a medium but I have a sister who is. Mediums are people who are born that way. They find it easy to make contact with the disembodied spirits that surround us and want to come close to us over the boundaries of flesh and blood. The medium has a control and through that control she makes the contacts. Can you come this evening?"

"This evening I have to be somewhere else."

"How about tomorrow?"

"Tomorrow I can come."

"Good! Be here tomorrow evening, and come with a feeling of trust, not doubt. Faith is potency and doubt is impotence. Do you understand?"

"A little, yes."

"Meanwhile, send your wife the first message. Close your eye and repeat after me, word for word: 'Rochelle, beginning today your power over me will begin to decline. Since you no longer love me, I have the right to find love elsewhere. I am determined to be free, independent, and no one can rob me of my freedom. All your attempts to keep me bound to you will fail. Our son is on my side—I find in him a friend and an ally.' "

With those last words something in Max's throat began to constrict. Each word he uttered had to break through a lump that had settled in his throat. He had to use all his strength to keep from howling.

"You can open your eyes now," Bernard Shkolnikov said. "Be here tomorrow at eight o'clock in the evening."

"How much do I owe you?" asked Max hesitantly.

"Five rubles. To take part in the séance it's three rubles." Max put his hands in his pants pocket and took out a banknote. Bernard Shkolnikov rose and Max followed suit.

"How did you learn all this, or did you study it somewhere?" Max asked.

"Oh, that's a long story. As a child I discovered forces in me that . . ."

Max Barabander said goodbye and Shkolnikov saw him to the door. Max looked at his watch. The hands showed that it had been only fifty minutes. Max went down the crooked steps.

"What is he? A thief, a crazy man, a magician?" Max asked himself. Whenever he had seen a nerve specialist, he had left with a feeling of despair. But this master of black magic who decorated his walls with monsters and flimflammery awakened in him a feeling of hope. Max felt close to both laughter and tears. Could this be true? Were his parents and Arturo alive and ready to help him?

It was good to come out in the open air, to feel the warmth of the sun. Max didn't take a droshky but walked until he came to Krasinski Garden. It smelled of grass and roses. Birds were twittering. "Where are all these souls?" Max asked himself. "How come only Shkolnikov's sister can bring them over?" But who knows what mysteries there are in this world?

Bernard Shkolnikov was right about one thing: Rochelle was carrying on a secret war with him. He often sensed that she was following him, watching him, teasing him. What did the clairvoyant call it? Magnetism.

Max came to a pond where swans were swimming and children were feeding them crumbs.

"If people don't die after death, then how about animals?" Max asked himself. "Every day millions of oxen, calves, sheep, chickens are slaughtered. Why don't their spirits return to choke the slaughterer? And what about soldiers who are killed in battle and Jews who are killed in pogroms?" Max said to himself.

He didn't believe in miracles, but Shmuel Smetena's calling

him today seemed like a miracle. Reading the newspaper and chancing upon that particular announcement in fine print was also out of the ordinary. Usually he did not read ads. What did he care about businesses in foreign countries?

Max had a lot of time left until five o'clock, but when you know you will be meeting someone in the evening you can relax and be alone. He went out on Nalewki Street and rambled through the Jewish streets. God in heaven, the signboards are in Yiddish letters, Yiddish was heard everywhere. He went into a huge courtyard, almost a city of its own, where men were loading wagons with boxes, barrels, and baskets, and market women were hawking their wares. He saw what looked like a studyhouse or a Hasidic synagogue, and went inside to take a look. Young boys with sidelocks were swaying back and forth over their Talmudic tomes, gesturing, explaining the meaning of these holy books to each other. In the middle of them an older man was saying Kaddish, not the usual prayer of mourning, but a different one with words that sounded strange to Max. Living abroad, he had got away from this old-fashioned Jewishness, but here they served God as in the old days in Roszkow. "Do they also believe in spirits? Then how come Shkolnikov shaves his beard—does he have another sort of belief?"

Max stood riveted by the door, unable to leave. A man with a yellow beard came up to him and asked, "You are here to pray? You can get a tallis and tefillin here. It's two kopecks!"

Max was silent for a while.

"I've already prayed. But here are two kopecks." He took out four rubles and gave it to him. "Everything revolves around rubles and kopecks," he said to himself. "Even in such a holy place." He went out, closing the door. At that moment he thought of Tsirele and remembered he had promised to see her father and get down to abc's.

From Dluga Street the droshky crossed over Tlomackie Street, passed Rymarska, Bankowy Square, coming out by the Iron Tower, and from there went to Gnoyna and Krochmalna Streets. The droshky passed an immense bank with huge pillars and a large courtyard. The bank looks like a fortress or a castle, Max thought. How many millions could be lying there? A closed, heavily armored wagon entered the gate and Max realized that it was loaded with money.

As soon as he came to Krochmalna Street, Max went right up to the rabbi's house. He had not planned it all out, but a scheme had evolved in his mind. He pushed the door open, went in, and found Tsirele and her mother.

Tsirele was wearing a white blouse which gave her a younger and fresher appearance. She was picking over sorrel leaves in a bowl. Seeing him she blushed and gave him a half-tearful, half-questioning look. I have bored my way in here like a worm, Max thought to himself. It was the kind of insight that the mind entrusts only to itself.

Apparently the rebbetzin was praying. In her hands she held her daily prayer book. Max said, "Good morning," and the rebbetzin nodded her head angrily. Her nose seemed pointed and sharp. From that one glance Max knew Tsirele had talked about him and the rebbetzin did not want him for her son-in-law. Her gray eyes looked at him with a kind of disgust.

Max was suddenly reminded of the word "untouchable."

"Mother and daughter, eh?" he said. "Continue praying, Rebbetzin, pray. Is the rabbi at home?"

"My father is in the other room," Tsirele answered.

"You're preparing dinner, ha? Here you still live as in the old days. What are you making? A sorrel borscht with potatoes?"

"Stay and eat with us," Tsirele said.

The rebbetzin mumbled something with her thin lips and made a sign that she could not speak. The sun reflected on her wig and lit up silken hairs of many hues. Max suddenly felt afraid of this woman. He sensed that even though she was observant and lived in a religious world, she thoroughly understood all his underhanded ways. It occurred to Max that she, too, might be a hot-blooded woman. She was surely not more than forty years old. Somehow he managed a wink to Tsirele.

He opened the door to the other room. The sun shone through the windows and the glass doors opening onto the balcony. The rabbi was standing at his lectern writing on a scrap of paper. The good man did not recognize him! How strange.

"What good tidings have you brought?"

"I am Max, Mordkhe, from America. You don't recognize me?"

"Hmm. Yes, of course, welcome."

The rabbi sat down at the head of the table and offered Max a seat.

"Rabbi, did I take you away from your studies?"

"No, no. Of course it's important to study. But as the saying goes, 'When studying the Torah becomes divorced from reality, there is no point in continuing.' It is said that if someone were only to repeat, 'The sister of Lotan was called Timno,' then he would fulfill the commandment to study Torah. Besides, hospitality to strangers is an important commandment. It's no small matter, a Jew, a Jewish face!" said the rabbi.

Max listened. The good man's words seemed to him full of grace. I must not harm these people, Max thought, and he said, "Rabbi, you are a very busy man, a holy man, and I am not worth the mud under your feet. I am a plain man, a crude person."

"God forbid, God forbid!"

"Listen, Rabbi. I am what I am. I went to cheder and my father—may he rest in peace—wanted to send me to yeshiva and all the rest. But I was drawn to back alleys, to the butcher's row. I'm telling you this so you won't be angry with me. I went into your house yesterday and as soon as I looked at your daughter I saw that the divine presence abides in her. That's what we used to say in Roszkow. She is beautiful, fine, as truly befits the daughter of a holy man. Her face is as radiant as the sun. Don't be angry with me, Rabbi. A man is a man. Even Moses was a man. I did study a little. I also said, Rabbi, that I was a widower. But before that I lost my child, an only son, a beloved, sheltered child. Then my wife passed away. It's been several years now that I've been wandering over the world. I go here, I go there. I have a lot of money. But what's the good of money when my heart is heavy? I know I'm not good enough to wash your feet and drink the water, but still I am a Jew. We are all, as they say, descended from one father. Rabbi, I am going to be my own *shadkhn*. Your daughter pleases me. I know I'm a lot older than her and I could be her father. But when a man is older, it is not considered such a bad thing. I would dress her in gold, handle her with kid gloves. It would be one God and one Tsirele. If I am speaking foolishly, Rabbi, please forgive me. I was never taught how to speak with a holy man." Max broke off.

The rabbi looked up and his eyes shone wondrously blue.

The cheeks over his red beard became flushed and he looked more like his daughter than ever. For a while he shook his head and his sidelocks shook too.

"Where do you plan to live? In faraway countries?"

"Rabbi, I'll go wherever you want. It's as if your words were written in the Bible. Warsaw is a great city. If I were to marry Tsirele, I would take her back with me for a trip to settle up all my businesses. It would take a few months or at most half a year. Why throw away good money? Houses would have to be sold or rented as well as lots and other property. I would put my entire fortune into gold bars, and after that I would come back here. Not just she, Rabbi, but you, too, would never be poor again. The rebbetzin wouldn't have to write out those receipts anymore. You would live in plenty and you would be able to study Torah without worry. May I be struck down if I am telling a lie."

"You must not swear! Don't swear!" the rabbi interrupted. "You musn't swear even on the truth. It is said that when God commanded, 'You must not take the name of the Lord in vain,' the whole world trembled."

"Well, Rabbi, I just want you to know that I am not telling fairy tales. Everything is absolutely accurate. I am indeed a plain man, but when it comes to something good, I am an expert. Even a peasant knows the difference between a sow's ear and a silk purse."

"Well, well, I understand," said the rabbi, as if to himself. "Such things shouldn't be done quickly, Such things must be discussed with members of the household. According to law, the girl must be asked, too. It is written: 'We must call in the maiden and ask her if she is willing.' "

"Of course, Rabbi, how else? If she doesn't like me, no

one will drag her to the wedding canopy. The rabbi should talk this matter over with the rebbetzin, Tsirele, and all. I know I don't deserve such a jewel, but I will be good to her. With me she will live like a countess. And with her the rabbi will be prosperous, too. My money will be your money. I will buy the children frock coats and whatever else they need. Krochmalna is not a good street. It's too crowded. We'll move to another street where the air is fresher and where there are trees and not so many boors and beggars. You'll be able to function as a rabbi, hold your court, if you wish, and if not, you can sit and study and you will be provided with the best and finest. I may sound like an ignoramus, but my thoughts are pure," said Max, marveling at his own words. He himself didn't know whether he was lying or whether he had blurted out the truth.

The rabbi lifted up his skullcap and fanned himself with it. "Can you conduct your business here?"

"My business is good anywhere. Besides, I have put away enough funds so that I can live on them for the next one hundred years. You put money in the bank and live on the interest. In Roszkow it was called 'cutting coupons.' Houses and lots are sold in every country. We would rent a whole floor with two big apartments and we would live next door to each other. I'll tell you something, Rabbi. I didn't descend out of thin air. My father—may he rest in peace—was a coachman, a pious Jew. When the rabbi from Turzysk came to Roszkow, he wanted to ride only in our *britska*, because he was afraid of—I forgot what it's called."

"*Shatnez.*"

"Yes, Rabbi. I forgot that word long ago, but you, Rabbi, remember it. Once he wanted to put a pillow behind him, so my father ripped open the seam and showed him that it was linen without wool. He wasn't a real student but he knew how to read the holy books. My mother—may she rest in peace— wore a cap on the Sabbath. We lived in one room but gave to God what belonged to God. When a stranger came to town, he ate with us. Everything was strictly kosher. I would swear, Rabbi, but swearing is not allowed. In America I moved away from Jewishness, but here, Rabbi, I am a Jew!" And Max began to thump on his chest with his middle finger. The rabbi looked at him kindly, amiably, full of family warmth.

"Everything is ordained," he said. "It is written that forty days before a person is born they call out, 'Daughter of such and such.' I sit and worry about where to get a dowry for my daughter and then you are sent here from far-off lands. My daughter is on the modern side," and here the rabbi's tone changed abruptly: "She reads the newspapers and this has led her to become enlightened. We wanted to make a match for her and a teacher's son."

"I know, Rabbi, with Reb Zaynvele."

The rabbi looked amazed. "How do you know?"

"I know, Rabbi, I know. As I live and breathe, I don't miss anything."

"They talk about her, then?"

"People have big mouths. But I said to them, If a girl says no, she mustn't be forced."

The rabbi clutched his beard and let it go. "We didn't force her. God forbid. But she is high-strung like her mother. Nerves are a sickness. One gets rattled and does things that one regrets later. Years ago it was called being tempted by evil. The Talmud says that a person doesn't sin unless a spirit of folly enters him. Well, there are choices and everything can be overcome if there is the will to do so. The doctors have called sins nerves and say that one doesn't have to do penance for a sickness. But that's a mistake. If a person wasn't capable of controlling his anger, then anger wouldn't be a sin."

"Yes, Rabbi, but a person could fly into a rage and be unable to get hold of himself. Where I live there was a Gentile, a Spaniard, and he had a wife and a mistress. His wife found out and she began to nag him. He already had children with the other one, too. In those countries it is an accepted thing. To make the story short, she bothered him so much that he took his rifle down from the wall and shot her and all the children to boot. After that he went to his mistress and did the same thing. One little girl of five hid under the bed and that's how she survived. When he tried to shoot himself, his rifle jammed, and he was taken to jail."

The rabbi knitted his brow. "Did they hang him?"

"No, they carried him off to the insane asylum."

"What did he accomplish? He will spend the rest of his life in a madhouse and in the other world there will be a day of reckoning. The blood that was spilled cries out from the earth and accuses the murderer. Does it make sense to do such a thing because of a moment's anger? How long does one live? We are sent here to do good, not evil."

Max sat silently for a while.

"Holy Rabbi, it's true. Every word you have uttered deserves to be kissed."

"If, with God's help, this turns out to be a match, I want you to be a Jew."

"What am I, then, a goy?"

"A Jew has to have a beard. Man is created in God's image, and the beard—"

"Whatever the rabbi says I'll do."

Suddenly there was a noise in the kitchen and the door to the rabbi's study opened. The rebbetzin poked the edge of her wig in the door.

When Max left the rabbi's house, it was not even one o'clock. He went down the steps slowly, taking out a handkerchief to wipe his brow. At the gate he remained standing for a while.

"What kind of mess am I cooking up?" he said to himself. "I'll divorce Rochelle. I won't drag that good man into the mud. If I do, I deserve to be cut to shreds." His eyes became moist and he felt close to tears. "God in heaven, punish me if I cause these good people shame. May Pharaoh's plagues descend upon me." Max began to head toward Gnoyna Street. The good man had told him to come back tomorrow, saying that he had to confer with the members of his household. Something in Max's head began to roar like a machine.

I won't go back there anymore, he decided. I'll break it off while there's still time! I won't go to Shmuel Smetena's either. I'll pack my things and go straight to Roszkow.

Max passed Senatorska Street, recognizing it by the tower of the City Council, and came out on Theater Square. Everything was as he remembered—the opera, Samedeni's Café. A huge open wagon arrived, full of decorations.

He went into a café and ordered coffee and cake. There were no Yiddish newspapers and a waiter brought him an illustrated journal, with photographs of a prince and princess who had just been married. Max was completely absorbed by the pictures. Four young pages were holding the train of her wedding dress and the groom wore a uniform with epaulettes. They were surrounded by men bedecked with medals and ladies in hats adorned with ostrich feathers, "Where is all this taking place—in Germany? Russia? England?" Suddenly everything began to swim before his eyes. He began to seethe with rage and, even though he himself had pursued the pleasures of the flesh, a kind of old-fashioned Jewish scorn for the world and its foolishness arose in Max. What was it they used to say in Roszkow? "Vanity of vanities." Everything is futile, empty; today you live, tomorrow you die. Are we chasing our own shadows? He took a look around at the men and women, young and old. Their faces had a greedy, troubled look. It seemed as if every one of them had made some kind of mistake and didn't know how to correct it. No matter how much they have, they are dissatisfied. If they have a hundred thousand rubles, they want a million. If they have one woman, they want three. Am I any different? Now, when I don't have anyone, I want to lead the rabbi's daughter astray. "Never in my life!" Max almost shouted out loud. "It's better to die!"

He paid the waiter and walked to the hotel. He thought he had forgotten the Warsaw streets but found his way easily: after New Senatorska Street, he turned into Trebacka Street and found himself not far from the hotel. He went up on the elevator and lay down on the bed in all his clothes. He had made up his mind not to go to Shmuel Smetena's, but at the same time he knew that he *would* go.

When he awoke, the clock showed twenty to four. "That Reyzl Kork will probably prepare a real feast," he said to himself. He put on a light-colored suit and an expensive shirt he had bought in Paris. What should he bring to this piece of goods? He must bring her something. He went down to the street and walked into a wine shop. When he saw a huge bottle of champagne, a magnum, the wine merchant began praising it as the best wine you could get. He asked a high price. Let's not go to anyone like a beggar, Max decided.

He became cheerful again. That's how things went lately. One moment he was sad, the next happy. He suddenly remembered the rabbi's words that nerves are the same thing as temptation to evil. "Oh, nonsense! What does such a man know about medicine? All he knows is to sway over his holy books. I won't go the rabbi anymore. The rebbetzin doesn't want me anyway. What's happening with me is nerves." One doctor had showed him a picture of a naked body completely threaded with nerves. "I should never have wormed my way into such a pious house," Max reproached himself. "Someone like Tsirele should marry her own kind."

When the clock moved closer to five, Max stepped into a droshky. Passersby stopped to look at him, all decked out with a big wine bottle wrapped in rose-colored paper. Max told the driver to go by way of Ciepla Street.

Going up the stairs, he smelled Reyzl Kork's meatballs. The door was opened by a woman with black hair, a fair face, large dark eyes, and a hooked nose. Seeing Max, her face broke into a smile. She began to talk to him in a warm, homey Polish Yiddish.

"What have you brought? My, oh my, just look at the size of the bottle! Champagne? I'm fainting away! Well, please come in."

She led Max into a room where the table was already set. The room contained a caged parrot and a huge sofa covered in maroon satin. On the wall were pictures of half-naked women and colorful landscapes. The apartment reminded Max of a high-class brothel and Reyzl Kork of a madam.

"Shmuel will be here soon," she said. "Give me your hat! What shall I do with the champagne?"

"You put it on ice."

"Good! I haven't drunk champagne in a hundred years!"

"How old are you, then, two hundred?" asked Max, striking the right note with her at once.

"Sometimes I feel I've been around a thousand years," Reyzl answered. Max liked the sound of her voice. It had the hoarseness of those who seek pleasure and never tire of it. "Here I feel at home," Max said to himself.

"Shmuel told me about meeting you and I was sorry I hadn't gone to that tavern. You should know that I have a sister in Buenos Aires."

"Where, on what street?"

"Yunin or Chunin Street, I don't know how it's pronounced."

"I know that street," said Max, and thought, Now I know what your sister's trade is.

Reyzl was a little heavy but not too fat. Her skin was exceptionally fair and smooth and her great sparkling eyes looked at a man with appetite and experience and without a trace of shame. With such a woman you could get right down to business. Her black hair was combed in an upsweep. Her neck and arms were bare and her skin was unwrinkled. Her mouth was meant to be kissed. Her pouting lips parted to reveal white teeth. She was wearing a black transparent dress.

"It's hot out, isn't it?" Max said.

"It's about time. We had a hard winter. Will you have a drink? I make my own lemonade and put in a little rum to give it flavor."

"I'll wait for Shmuel."

"He should have been here by now. But with him you never know. He walks down the street and is stopped by the police sergeant, or even by the commissar himself. People run after him and they all want favors. You have to be made of iron, and now the doctors are advising him to go to Marienbad."

"What's wrong with him?"

"He has a bad heart. He can lift four hundred pounds but he goes up a few stairs and starts to wheeze."

"He's not young anymore."

"A man is always young. It depends on who he's with."

Max almost said, "You're a corker." He had a sudden desire to take her in his arms.

"How is it going for you, sister, good?" he asked.

Reyzl sat on the edge of her chair, facing Max on the sofa.

"Not bad. My servant girl is whipping some eggs into the borscht and I must see that it doesn't curdle. I hear you sell houses."

"Houses and lots. Buenos Aires is growing. Where five years ago there was a field or a lawn, today there is a street. I had a tragedy in my life. My son—"

"I know, I know."

"How do you know?"

"My sister wrote me a letter. We received it yesterday."

"Your sister knows me?"

"Yes, she does. Have you ever heard of Madame Shay-evsky? There she is called Señora."

"No, I don't know her."

"But she knows you. She wrote that you might be coming to Warsaw and that I should get acquainted with you. It's a small world, isn't it?"

"It's really amazing."

"Shmuel comes and tells me about meeting you and the very next day a letter arrives—again about you. If that's how it is, I thought, then I'd better have a look at this man."

"What can you see by just looking?"

"I see everything."

"What do you see?"

"That I will tell you another time. We'll have a chance to talk and talk. If you fall into my hands it's not so easy to get out of them," said Reyzl with a smile and a wink as she got up. "Let me see what she's doing with my borscht."

"Well, this is a woman and a half," he said to himself. He wondered which he wanted more, the meatballs and the borscht, or the lady of the house. He had just said to Reyzl that he was not thirsty, but his throat now felt dry.

Max went to the window and looked into the courtyard. Children were playing a game of tag, *palant*—a kind of paddleball—and *klipa*. A girl was tossing a rubber ball in the air with two sticks bound with string and catching it, a *diabol*. He heard Reyzl opening the front door and became aware of sounds and talk in the corridor. Shmuel Smetena had arrived.

After they had eaten, Shmuel Smetena said he had to lie down. He was tired and had eaten and drunk too much. Reyzl walked him into the bedroom. He stretched out on the bed in his clothes and began to snore immediately.

The servant girl removed the dishes. Reyzl poured herself some liqueur in a small glass. Max half reclined against the sofa. The setting sun threw purple shadows on the wall and on Reyzl's face.

Reyzl talked about her sister and little by little led the discussion around to the matter in hand. Her sister, Señora

Shayevsky (her first name was Feygele or Fanya), had a salon where men came to enjoy themselves. Of course the girls got older or faded, and from time to time one of them got married. Occasionally a girl took to drink. Men were like children, always in need of new toys, new dolls. Reyzl knew lots of young girls in Warsaw, she knew beauties. In Warsaw they couldn't get mixed up with men because they lived with their families. But if they had an opportunity to get out of the country, to dress in beautiful clothes and so on, you could easily convince them. The main point was that everything must be done skillfully. But for such a business you needed a man. Shmuel Smetena wasn't any good at it; he knew how to talk to a commissar but not to a pretty girl.

"They always talk about girls being abducted. Nonsense! It's no longer a matter of abduction. Girls are walking around here who want to see the world, but they have no money to foot the bill. They can't even get decent jobs as servants. And as to getting married, not a chance," Reyzl said.

"Why not?"

"The least little tailor wants a dowry. A clerk on Gesia Street who scrapes together twelve rubles a week wants to be paid in gold." As it grew darker and darker, Reyzl's face became full of shadows. Only her eyes glowed in the twilight, large dark eyes alight with sparks.

"If I were a man, I would turn the world on its head," Reyzl said.

"What would you do?"

"What wouldn't I do? A man can go everywhere, say whatever he wants, make a proposition to anyone who catches his eye. The two of us could make a fortune."

"Doesn't Shmuel give you enough?"

"People are pigs."

Then she began to talk directly and indirectly. She could procure women if Max would just talk them into it. Her sister, Señora Shayevsky, knew which doors were open. Money was no object and the market was enormous. People were looking for beautiful girls everywhere—in Argentina, in Brazil—wherever men travel without their families. Naturally, with each respectable girl you have to talk differently. While you can show your hand to some, others want to be sweet-talked. You almost have to pretend to be in love with them. A real man knows which woman to kiss and which to slap. As soon as a girl finds herself in a foreign country, without a passport, without a penny, rendered dumb, she will do whatever you want. The police could be bribed. The main thing was to get the woman over the border and booked on a ship. The rest was easy.

"My sister is right," Reyzl said. "You're the person to handle this."

"Why didn't she come to me in Buenos Aires?"

"Your wife doesn't let anyone near you."

"Well, that's true."

Max lit a cigarette. When he struck the match, for a moment he saw Reyzl's face. She looked serious, even a bit fearful. Max knew very well that his answer should be that he was too old, had no need of money, had other things to worry about. But it was good to sit with this woman, her voice stroking him. She spoke about men with a kind of girlish enthusiasm that seemed out of keeping for an experienced person. But who knows what goes on in someone else's head? thought Max. A woman can have a hundred men and remain a foolish little girl.

"What do you know about Tsirele, the rabbi's daughter?" Max inquired.

"Run away from her as you would from fire."

"Why?"

"She's not our kind. She fell in love with a striker, Vova. They killed him in a demonstration, and when she heard the news she fainted. She believes in—what do you call it?—a constitution."

"I would take her to Argentina."

"It's a waste of money."

Reyzl explained everything. For this shady business you needed beautiful girls from common families, girls who couldn't sign their names, not radicals, or the shmintelligentsia who had big mouths that could send them to the gallows. During the strikes, these girls sat in garrets and made bombs. While one girl was making a bomb, it went off and blew off her legs. Why should they get involved in such a hopeless situation? Reyzl herself had two or three girls with whom Max could come to an understanding right now. These were young women who were growing up poor and defenseless. If they went to work in factories, they contracted consumption. Besides, the factories didn't like to hire Jewish girls. Even Jewish bosses wanted Gentile girls. *Reyferkes*, the women who find positions for servant girls, always had ten girls for each job. The ugly ones usually had no chance, but if a girl was pretty, she didn't have to suffer.

"When can I look at the merchandise?" Max asked.

"It could even be tonight."

"How will the cat come over the water?"

"Hush." In the twilight he saw Reyzl putting a finger to her lips. She got up and looked into the bedroom. After a while she closed the door. "He'll continue to snore like that until morning."

Max got up, too. He went over to Reyzl and put his hands on her hips.

"You're a pretty nice piece of goods."

"I was once."

"Now, too."

"Shmuel considers me cheap merchandise."

Max bent over and kissed Reyzl on the lips. She embraced him and ate into his mouth, kissing and biting at the same time. He said, "Well, so be it."

"Yes, my dear, the two of us can do great things together."

He led her backward toward the sofa, his knees pushing against hers.

Reyzl pulled away from him. "Not like this."

"How then?"

"Even though he's snoring, he could be eavesdropping. He has the soul of a spy," Reyzl whispered, and giggled. She had been faithful to Shmuel for twelve years. Men chased her but she wasn't interested in any of them. The riffraff, the loafers on the street, awakened disgust in her. There were no decent men on Krochmalna Street. Once an actor from the Yiddish theater had attached himself to her, but all he wanted was to talk about himself and show off. Shmuel Smetena had once been a strong man but he was already past sixty. He had a paunch from drinking too much beer.

"At my age money is preferable to romance," said Reyzl.

"Yes, you don't get younger, just older."

Max had heard the very same words from his father, but his father had used them in the sense that one must be a good man and not sin. He urged his son to do penance, especially in the month of Elul, when every fish in the water trembles and

Jews go to say their penitential prayers in anticipation of the High Holidays. But Reyzl's intent was to provide herself with money. Max's fantasies were Reyzl's practical plans. She wanted him to get women to go to Argentina. She would become his partner; his lover, too. She would help him. She had already given him a kiss that aroused him. Max forgot all his weaknesses, obsessions, and fears. She was standing beside him at the sofa and holding his wrists with a force that is seldom found in women. She exuded feminine power and intoxicating promises.

"I will come to you," she whispered in his ear, and bit his earlobe.

"When?"

"One of those girls is a servant here in this court. If you'd like, I'll tell her to come in."

"What about the people she works for?"

"They're not at home."

"*Bueno.*"

Max sat down on the sofa. He heard Reyzl pick up the telephone in the corridor. It was completely dark except for the light that shone in from the windows on the opposite wall. He had the feeling that he had been through this before. He knew full well that Reyzl was dragging him into the mire. He didn't need the money and he thought he had made up his mind to lead a respectable life, but this Reyzl was a ball of fire. Perhaps she could release him from the magic spell of impotence he suffered from. She would procure others for him as well. Something would happen here. Warsaw wasn't London or Berlin, where he had traipsed around all alone. Thank God, here people were running after him, not the other way around. Tomorrow the rabbi had to give him an answer. Tsirele was waiting for him. He had kissed the baker's wife but had not slept with her, and now he could have Reyzl Kork. Tomorrow he would be seeing Bernard Shkolnikov, and his sister would call up the spirit of the dead.

Max sat enveloped in darkness. "What can I lose?" he remonstrated with himself. "It can't be worse for me than it is. Even prison is better than wandering about free and not being able to enjoy anything. Even death is better . . ." The neighborhood youngsters in the courtyard had apparently stopped playing ball. Silence seeped in through the windows. Max saw a strip of sky and a few stars. He heard steps and Reyzl came in.

"The girl will be here right away. We'll talk in the kitchen."

It had all the earmarks of a conspiracy. Max got up and went toward Reyzl. He had to be careful not to bump into the edge of a table or a chair. At the door he put his hands on Reyzl's shoulders. "When will you come to see me?"

"Hush! He has to go to Lodz soon. He has a job to do there."

As much as Max derived pleasure from this stealthy secret, somewhere deep down it also troubled him. As corrupt as he was, hidden somewhere in him there was an honest man, a moralizer who terrorized him with thoughts of the day of death and the hell to come. This had begun right after Arturo's death and it never left him. Could it all be coming from Rochelle's magnetism, as Bernard Shkolnikov had said? It seemed rather that it was his father talking to him with a hidden strength right from the grave.

Reyzl called out to him and he went into the kitchen, a big room with a tile floor and copper pans on hooks. A young girl with fiery red hair, green eyes, and a face covered with freckles was sitting on a kitchen bench. She had a snub nose and thick lips. Reyzl Kork had said she was pretty but Max saw no beauty in her. Neither was she ugly, he thought. If she could only scrape those freckles off her face! She was wearing a calico dress and a shawl over her shoulders. There was an air of friendly provinciality about her. Could she be from Roszkow? Max wondered. He took a quick look at her shoes. They were full of holes and were fastened with buttons.

"Panye Barabander, this is the girl."

"What's your name?"

"Basha."

"Where are you from, Basha?"

"From Opole."

"Opole, eh? I have heard of that town. What does your father do?"

"A wheeler-dealer," said the girl, half smiling.

"Do you have any brothers and sisters?"

"Three brothers and two sisters. I am the oldest."

"How old are you, then?"

"Nineteen."

"You look sixteen. Does everyone in your family have red hair or are you the only one?"

"Me and one little brother."

"Would you like to get away from Russia?" Max asked, not sure whether he should have come to the point so quickly. The girl answered right away.

"What do I have here? I work the whole season and they give me eight rubles. If I go home for the holidays and buy a dress or a present, the money is gone. My mistress says that in America they pay well and a servant girl can save up for a dowry. I don't want to be a servant forever. My mistress bosses me around the whole day and I can't even go to sleep when I want to. They get up late, but I have to be up before dawn and on my feet at six in the morning."

"Sit down, Max, don't stand," said Reyzl, pushing a chair under him.

"Here it's still like it was thirty years ago," Max started to say. "Everything has remained old-fashioned. Abroad life has changed. For example, why do you need a shawl on such a hot day? And shoes with high tops are not in style for the summer when it's hot. There people don't ask you what you are and who you are. A girl is called a señorita and when you get married you're a señora. The people who went to Argentina weren't from high society. A father might have been a thief, but his daughter lives in high style and is the leader of her social circle. Nobody wears a wig or a cap like they do here. It's all fanaticism from King Sobieski's times. Why cut off your own hair and wear the hair of a woman who may have already died? And that's how it is with everything. They wrote things in the holy books that are made up out of whole cloth. Nobody eats kosher anymore where I live. Maybe there's a ritual slaughterer somewhere, but just try and find him. What does the ox care how he's killed? Everything is advanced there and a girl isn't afraid of a man. In my country there are more men than women and a woman is treated with respect. The main thing is not to be backward and to forget Grandma's prayer books."

Max kept talking as if he knew it all by heart. His own words captivated him. Reyzl Kork's face was full of smiles, her eyes sparkled. He seemed to have read her mind. He had said exactly what was needed.

Basha took off her shawl, smiling shyly.

"Yes, it's true. You ought to see what it's like in Opole," she replied. "There it's still like a hundred years ago. I come home for the holidays and the fights start. My mother wants me to go to the women's shul. But I'm tired of standing on my feet all day. The rich women sit on the bench and we must stand."

"Well, I see that you are a girl of good sense. If you want to come with me, don't tell anybody anything. People begrudge others. They have husbands and children and can't move anymore and they want everyone else to remain stuck in the mud. If you want to go abroad, you must get a passport, which costs twenty-five rubles. That's for the rich who travel to the spas, not your kind. We'll get you across the border and then you won't need any passport. You'll be put on a ship and we'll get you off and take care of you. I myself have a business, and if you don't work out there, we'll place you somewhere else. We'll take off all those rags and dress you like a princess with a hat, a purse, and a pretty cape. We have certain creams that you can put on that will take off freckles. You must have skin as white as milk. Lift up your sleeve. Let me take a look."

Basha hesitated for a while. Then she pushed up her sleeve. Max looked at her arm like an expert.

"What did I say? White as snow. You weren't vaccinated against smallpox? You don't have any marks."

"Smallpox? I don't know. No."

"That's Russia for you. Over there, just as soon as a child is born, he's vaccinated. They won't let you on the ship unless you are vaccinated. But I will take care of everything. You must remember one thing—silence. If you say one word to anyone, you will spoil everything."

"Who would I talk to? I don't hide anything from this woman here. She knows all my secrets."

"Were you ever engaged or anything?"

"To nobody. The boys bother me but I give them what for. They think that just because I'm a poor girl, they can take advantage of me. On the Sabbath they go to shul with the boss, but in the middle of the week they are big dandies."

"Good! Behave decently. If someone wants to take, they have to give. We have a saying, 'For nothing, you can go only to the bathhouse.' And in Warsaw you can't even go to the bathhouse for nothing. You understand what I am getting at?"

"Yes, I understand."

"If you don't act like a fool, you'll be eating in the tabernacle."

"When are you leaving?" Basha asked after some reflection.

"It will take a little while yet. Perhaps several weeks or a few months, but we'll go. Till then play dumb. Reyzl will inform you of everything. If I need you I'll come here. I hear that the old man has a telephone. Give me the number. What are you doing on the Sabbath?"

"Oh, I have to bring back the *cholent* from the baker. They don't let me wash the dishes because there's no hot water, but I have to clear off the dishes. For the last meal of the Sabbath they get hungry and I have to bring sour milk."

"Can you get away for a few hours?"

"Maybe. Yes."

"I'll meet you somewhere and we'll go to the theater, or to a pastry shop. I'll buy you a dress and whatever you need. That will be on credit. When you earn, you'll pay me back."

"You are a good person."

"I'm not good, I'm doing it for my own reasons. I have businesses and we need people. There's no lack of men, but for certain kinds of work, only girls are suitable. The essential thing is to do what you are told. When you go with me, then I am your father, your mother, your sister, your fiancé. All you have to do is obey and everything will be just fine."

"Yes, I understand."

"What do you say?"

"I hope something will come of it."

"Something *will* come of it. The main thing is to keep your mouth shut. If you say one word to anyone, even your best girl friend, then right away there's talk and the whole thing falls apart. Here, take this ruble!" and Max took out his wallet. Basha inclined her head.

"Why this ruble?"

"For your pretty eyes. To you a ruble is a fortune. To me it's of no importance. You'll pay me back. I won't lose any money because of you. I'm writing it down in my little book and there it will stay. Buy yourself a pair of stockings or whatever you need. Would you be able to meet me on the Sabbath at one o'clock?"

"One o'clock is too early. By the time they finish singing the Sabbath songs and saying the benedictions, it's often two o'clock."

"Is three o'clock good?"

"Three, yes."

"*Bueno.* Meet me at three on Ciepla Street. There's a barracks there; meet me across the street. I'll be there at three sharp and we'll talk everything over. Here's the ruble."

"Oh, thank you."

"Take it and use it in good health. We're people, not animals."

"Should I go now?"

"You can go now," Reyzl answered. "But don't forget to

be there on the Sabbath at three o'clock across from the barracks. Don't let the man wait for you, and let it be a secret among the three of us. We won't do you any harm, God forbid."

"Good night. Be well."

"Good night."

As soon as Basha had closed the door, Reyzl ran over to Max and embraced him, pressing him to her.

"Mother mine, you're some fellow. The way you talk, every word merits a kiss. Where did you get such a smooth tongue? If that girl doesn't melt from happiness, she is stronger than iron. With your mouth you could seduce the Tsarina herself!"

"She's already been seduced. It's all in the papers; what's his name? Rasputin!"

"What do you think of the girl?"

"Not such a beauty."

"A pure virgin. If you dressed her up, her own mother wouldn't recognize her. A fresh piece of goods. I have prettier ones, too. What do they have there? Old whores."

"If only she doesn't spill everything."

"She'll be quiet as a dog. You should know that I already prepared her. But what takes me weeks, you do in ten minutes. You hit the mark, you touch their hearts. What will you do with her on the Sabbath? Seduce her?"

"So quickly?"

"Someone like you can do anything. Can I use the familiar *thou* with you? You were talking with her and I became jealous. I actually need you here in Warsaw."

"Come with me to Argentina."

"And what will happen to Shmuel? He knows everybody, has all the right connections. Take him out of Warsaw and he's a nobody."

"Leave him here."

"Oh? Maybe; yes. He has a wife. Something will happen between us. You're my type. What would I do in Buenos Aires?"

"We would stay half a year there, and half a year here."

"May this come true! If we work together, we'll rake in gold. Wait, I'll take a look and see if Shmuel is sleeping."

When Reyzl Kork went out, Max lit up a cigarette. "Well, it's all just a game. I'm not going to become a pimp in my old age." Max inhaled the smoke deeply. He had made all this talk just to impress Reyzl, to show her how much power he had over the female sex. Let the girl have a ruble. She was a poor child. Max knit his brows. Thoughts were spinning in his head. If this Reyzl could break the spell, he would take her with him. How was she worse than Rochelle? A lot better! Shmuel would find someone else. After all, on Krochmalna Street he was king.

Something awoke in Max which in modern parlance is called conscience. He was afraid that he might hurt someone. He kept on justifying himself. How did this happen? There was a time when he hurt people and it hadn't bothered him. He had grown up with the idea that you could do what you wanted with a woman. He always went by the adage that all is fair in love and war. All of a sudden something in him had softened. He wanted to make amends for every sin—with money, with words, with presents. An aversion arose in him against all those who take nothing into account except their own desires, like Reyzl Kork. She would surely have sold her own mother for a few rubles. Could it be that all this had come from Arturo's death, or was he, Max, sick with a hidden illness?

Reyzl returned. "He's sleeping like a dead man. But with him you never know. All of a sudden he can wake up and surprise you."

"When is he going to Lodz?"

"Next week."

"How long will he stay there?"

"A few days."

"Will you come to me?"

"Yes, you to me or me to you."

ax Barabander slept soundly until he was awakened by an attendant knocking on his door: "Telephone call!" He quickly put on his bathrobe and slippers. It was nearly 10 a.m. Who could it be, Max wondered, Reyzl Kork?

He was about to say "Reyzele, how are you?" when he heard another woman's voice. But she spoke hesitantly, almost stammering. It was Tsirele, the rabbi's daughter.

"Did I wake you up?" she asked.

"No, Tsirele, it's almost ten."

"My father wants to speak with you."

"Well, good. When shall I come? Does he consent?"

"Oh, I haven't slept the whole night."

"What did they decide?"

"Come over. They will tell you everything."

"When shall I come?"

"Whenever you want. My father is in the prayerhouse now, praying. After that he will be at home."

"Tsirele, why are you hoarse?" asked Max.

"Oh, it's a miracle!"

"Hm, good. I'll come over soon."

"When?"

"I'll be there by noon."

"My father agreed right away, but my mother is a nervous woman . . . a worrier. I talked my heart out. I made it crystal-clear: 'I'm not going to marry a yeshiva boy.' I was ready to pack my bag and run away."

"Run away where?"

"To you."

"Well, I'll be there."

Max hung up the receiver and remained standing as if possessed. Was it possible? Yes, everything is possible. Yet he felt no joy. On the contrary, he was seized with dread. "What will I do with her?" he asked himself as he returned to his room. "I can't get involved with Reyzl Kork, neither can I take Tsirele with me, because I have a wife. For a sin committed against that good man, God will punish me. What's actually keeping me here in Warsaw? Am I staying in order to meet with Shkol-nikov so he can put me in touch with the dead? Or to eat meatballs and dried egg barley again with Reyzl Kork?"

He looked at his valises. It would take no more than five minutes to pack up, settle his account, take a droshky to the Vienna Station, and get into a first-class train. They wouldn't try to follow him. Well, he could take the train tomorrow, too. On the other hand, where would he go? Back to Buenos Aires, heading right into winter? The truth was that for him the whole world now seemed hollow. "Shall I go to Roszkow? What will I do there?" His relatives had probably forgotten his name by now, and surely most of them had died.

Yes, there's always time to run away, Max reasoned. We'll play a little yet. He began to wash, shave, and put on his clothes. The morning was mild and sunny and for a while Max stood by the window looking out at the passersby. Everyone has his destiny. At the age of forty-seven, it was Max's fate to wander about without a purpose. He got dressed and went outside. It was better to be involved in wild ventures than to sit on a bench in Whitechapel and strike up a conversation with a missionary, as he had done in England. This time Max had coffee in a café on Cracow Suburbs Street. After that he went on foot toward Krochmalna Street. By now he knew the way and even recognized the smells. When he came to Krochmalna Street, his watch showed exactly twelve o'clock.

He went upstairs to the rabbi and found Tsirele, pale as if after a sickness, dressed up in a white blouse and in a light-green skirt. She was sitting on the bed and mending a stocking that she had stretched over a glass. At a table the rebbetzin was shelling peas. On the way upstairs, Max had been seized by a bridegroom's bashfulness, as if he had just come from Roszkow and was going to view his bride. But he braced himself and threw off his shyness. He had money, a passport stamped with visas, a gold watch in his vest pocket, and packed in his baggage there was a revolver.

"Good day, Rebbetzin; good day, Tsirele," Max said. "Is the rabbi at home?"

Tsirele looked at him sideways, frightened. The rebbetzin turned her pointed face toward him, her gray eyes piercing him with a look of regret and curiosity. Wrinkles appeared above her nose. "In the other room."

Max knew he should say something to these women. But what? He, the big talker, had run out of words. He went into the prayerhouse and found the rabbi just as he was yesterday. In a skullcap, faille caftan, standing by the lectern and writing on a scrap of paper. This time the good man called out, "Welcome."

"Holy Rabbi!"

"Sit, sit. Right here . . ." And the rabbi sat down at the head of the table.

Max took a look at the bookshelves, at the Holy Ark with its curtains, the lions, the Ten Commandments, and he was seized with the same humility he had felt the day before. "Could there be any greater honor than becoming the son-in-law of this rabbi?" Max said to himself. "I'll worship the ground she walks on. I'll kiss her like a mezuzah."

In this house an air of tranquillity reigned that he had not experienced in any other country or any other place, not even in the museums in Paris, London, and Berlin. The whole world was marked by haste, competition, and alienation. Here everything was leisurely, intimate, agreeable. An otherworldly goodness peered out of this man's blue eyes. Flecks of sunlight played upon the gold-papered walls, the table, the bookcases. The room smelled of tea, lemon, and the Sabbath spice box.

"Reb Mordkhe," the rabbi said, "I talked everything over with my wife and with the members of my household. I will tell you the truth. My spouse and I would like to make a match with a young man, a scholar, but it's difficult. I have no dowry for her. Well, my daughter is a bit modern. And what can you do? It's another generation, other customs. In heaven they surely know what's happening. In short, we consent—with one condition: You must let your beard grow in, because a beard is a symbol of Jewishness. You must promise us that you will keep kosher, not violate the Sabbath, and observe all the religious laws. If you don't know a law, I have a little book where every-thing is written down in Yiddish so you can read it. The author is my father-in-law's relative by marriage, Reb Isaiah Rakhover, who wanted to do something for the people. Not everyone can read Hebrew, but the main thing is to conduct yourself as a Jew. We would, of course, want you to live here because she is our only daughter and we wouldn't want her to be far away in distant lands. It so happens that I am a rabbinical judge and as long as you don't have a beard, I can't write the engagement contract, because if I accept a son-in-law who has shaved his beard in violation of Jewish law, then it means that it pleases me. The Gemara says, Silence is consent. Therefore it would be a good idea if we would agree orally until your beard grows in, and then, with God's help, we will write the engagement contract and set the date for the wedding. Those short clothes of yours aren't to my liking either, because that is imitating the Gentiles. Since the Gentiles and the Germans dress in short clothes, then it behooves a Jew to dress in long clothes. But that is as you wish. You can also be a Jew in a short jacket. The essential thing is that a Jew must keep the laws. If not, he is violating the Torah, and what are Jews without the Torah? How did we withstand all our tribulations for almost two thousand years? Only because the Torah taught and strengthened us. A Jew without Torah is worse than a Gentile . . . You understand, ha?"

"Yes, Holy Rabbi, I understand."

"Do you agree?"

"Whatever the holy man says is so. Your word is as if God were talking to me."

"God forbid! A person is no more than flesh and blood, but what I tell you is taken from the Torah. If you wish, I will study a passage from the Talmud with you. You can begin with the Pentateuch. There is no greater moral tract than the Pentateuch. From the very first verse, it is full of moralizing. For as soon as the One on High created heaven and earth, people had to serve Him and obey His commandments. Rashi says, right in the first commentary, that the Almighty created heaven and earth because of the Jews and the Torah. It is said that the Almighty created the world out of the letters of the Torah."

"Holy Rabbi, I'm not worth the dust under your shoes."

"Here now, what kind of talk is that? We are all children of Abraham, Isaac, and Jacob. An ordinary Jew can be a saintly man. It has been affirmed that the Thirty-six Secret Saints are simple people—shoemakers, tailors, water carriers. My daughter is a little bit impulsive, but she has a good heart. She is a compassionate woman, and because of that she sometimes says things that she shouldn't, reproaches the Master of the Universe because there are poor people. How can we know the ways of the Almighty? All is ordained from above. Wait a moment, excuse me. I will call in the members of my household."

The rabbi went into the kitchen. Max rose. He went over to the bookcase and took out a holy book. It was printed entirely in Rashi type. "What does it say?" He tried to read but didn't understand anything. He could read only the permission printed in Russian by the censor on the title page. Max pulled out a second book and a third book. "I'll never be a student."

He had an urge to go out on the balcony, but he didn't want the neighborhood rabble to gossip. He knew he had no business being involved with either Reyzl Kork or Tsirele. A beard? The very thought made him laugh. Maybe Shkolnikov's dead will tell me what to do. He heard murmuring from the kitchen, suppressed and hasty speech. Suddenly he remembered that Reyzl Kork's sister, Señora Shayevsky, knew about his wife and therefore knew that he was not a widower. They could arrest him even in Warsaw for trying to marry someone when he already had a wife. "I'm driving myself into a trap that I'll never get out of!"

The door opened. Leading the way was the rabbi, followed by the rebbetzin, and behind her Tsirele.

After Max came out of the rabbi's house, he stood on the steps awhile. The rabbi had used the familiar *thou* to him. The rebbetzin had wished him *mazel tov*. Because of his beardlessness, the engagement contract had been postponed, but Max promised that he would soon go to Roszkow and wait there until his beard grew in.

He was making a fool not only of Tsirele but also of the good man and his wife. She, too, was a rabbi's daughter. Max said to himself, "One death is not enough. I should be cut to ribbons!" He started walking down the street. He turned his head and saw Tsirele on the balcony. She was gazing at him, shaking her head, making a motion as if she was sending him a kiss. "The wicked Haman was a saint in comparison with me . . . Such deeds God punishes, right in this world."

He hadn't been drinking but he was swaying as if he were drunk. His legs became limp, the stones of the sidewalk rocked under him. The summer day still stretched ahead of him and Max didn't know what to do with himself. Shkolnikov he would see in the evening. Go into a tavern and really get drunk? Go back to the hotel? He had no desire for whiskey, nor was he able to sit alone in his hotel room with his befuddled thoughts.

Max looked with envy at the passersby. Their lives were honest, not like his, a tangle of lies and swindles. If only he could end it all. He had a revolver in his valise. All he had to do was put it to his temple and press the trigger. As if of their own accord, his feet led him back to the hotel.

What's today? Yes, Thursday. On the Sabbath he was meeting with the red-haired girl Basha. Reyzl Kork was supposed to telephone him when Shmuel Smetena was leaving for Lodz. He lay down on the bed and looked at the ceiling. Around the hook (the very same one from which Max considered hanging himself) flies were aimlessly circling and buzzing. What joy suddenly possesses them? Max wondered. Is it a kind of fly's dance or a fly wedding?

Through the open window a summer breeze wafted in odors of trees, grass, horse manure, fields. Perhaps he would go for a swim in the Vistula. Max remembered a pool in the river where in the past you could take a swim. Now he was not in the mood for bathing. He was also afraid to leave his passport, clothes, and wallet on the riverbank. Who knows what thieves would do!

He had an urge to take out his revolver, but he decided that he shouldn't fool around with such a destructive weapon. The revolver could sometimes discharge by itself. In Russia carrying a weapon was forbidden. The longer Max ruminated, the clearer it became to him that aside from the fact that the whole situation was bad news, this was going to be a lost day. He had no place to go, nothing to do. If only there was a casino where he could lose a few rubles!

Max began to fall asleep. He imagined that he was winning thousands, hundreds of thousands of francs in Monte Carlo. He visualized the roulette tables, the croupiers, the other players, especially a woman with white hair who stretched out a hand with crippled fingers covered with diamonds and shouted, "I'm staking everything, the entire estate my husband left me." She piled stacks of gold coins on the table. "How can an old witch like that carry so much money around with her?" Max asked himself. "And how had that husband of hers put together such a hoard? Not from reciting psalms . . ." Max awoke with a start and sprang up with a shudder. "What did I dream?" he asked himself.

He recalled his bold words to the rabbi, the rebbetzin's warnings, quiet reproaches, and insinuations concerning the fact that he was uneducated and not worthy of becoming the husband of a rabbi's daughter, Tsirele's imploring looks. It all left him with a bitter taste in his mouth. "What do I need this for? What kind of devilish game have I got into?" He remembered his mother's words: *A person is his own worst enemy . . . Ten enemies can't do what a person does to himself.*

"Well, *adieu*, Warsaw!" Max said out loud. "I'm leaving you right away." He looked at his luggage. "I'll go wherever my eyes take me. I'll catch the first train!"

Someone knocked at the door. When Max opened it, there stood a hotel clerk and a man dressed in civilian clothes who was wearing a derby, a *melonik*, as it was called in Warsaw, and a checked suit. "When are you leaving?" he said. "We must get your room ready."

"What's this about leaving?" Max asked, stunned.

"You were supposed to leave today by twelve noon."

"Why?"

"I'm afraid there's been a mistake," the clerk said, and began to study a paper he was holding in his hand. The person in the derby hat smiled obsequiously and even seemed to wink. The clerk said, "I'll go down and clear everything up," and then he shut the door without apologizing.

"What's this? They're throwing me out of here?" Max asked himself. For days he had had the suspicion that they were taking a dim view of him at the hotel. Bellhops and chambermaids kept knocking at the door and even putting their keys in the keyhole and opening it while he was in the room. They apologized mockingly, under their breaths. Perhaps someone had informed against him to the authorities. But what could they have accused him of? He hadn't come to Warsaw with any contraband.

Max began to pace around the room. He had severed his ties with the underworld, but he had never really got used to the world of the wealthy, the aristocrats, the industrialists, the elegant ladies. He felt he was looked at with suspicion everywhere—in London, in Paris, in Berlin. In Buenos Aires his Polish accent in Spanish gave him away. The rebbetzin had jabbed him with harsh words. He must become a better kind of man; it's never too late to learn, to become more refined. She hinted openly that he was a boor and that she was giving him her daughter because Tsirele was not quite respectable, having tried to commit suicide.

Again Max heard a knock at the door. "Do they want to throw me out?" When he opened it, there was Tsirele. He looked at her, stunned. She was wearing a light-colored suit and the straw hat he had bought her. He had never seen her look so elegant. Nobody would have taken her to be the daughter of a rabbi; she could just as well be a countess. Max was suffused with joy and shame. Is it over her that I'm agonizing? I'd give my last groschen to be with her! he thought.

"Come in! Come in!" and he began to kiss her. Tsirele struggled with him: "Not here!"

He brought her into his room, and when he started kissing her again, he felt the sharp prick of a hatpin. He threw himself on his knees and clasped her feet. Tsirele laughed and scolded: "Get up! What's wrong with you?"

"Tsirele, you are my God!"

"What are you saying? You mustn't talk that way!"

"My life is yours!"

He got up and took her in his arms. He swayed with her and kissed her neck, her shoulders, her sleeves, her gloved hands. From now on and forever he would live only for Tsirele. He would divorce Rochelle even if it cost him three-quarters of his fortune.

Tsirele could barely wrest herself from his arms. "Oh, you are a wild man."

"God himself sent you to me."

"I wanted to talk everything over. I tried to telephone but they told me you had moved out."

"What kind of craziness is that? I'm going down to the clerk this minute and give him what for. Such dolts!"

"Don't get excited! If my mother knew that I came to visit you, she would flay me alive. But I told her I was going to the doctor. We have a Dr. Frankel who knows my father. He writes in Hebrew for *Ha-Zefirah* and talks to him about the Gemara. He won't take any money from us."

"Why do you need to see a doctor?"

"My mother says that I look pale. I've gotten into the habit of waking up in the middle of the night and can't close my eyes anymore."

"With me you'll sleep well."

"Oh, how you talk! You ought to be ashamed!" And Tsirele blushed from her neck up to her forehead.

"Why are you embarrassed? Man and wife sleep together."

"Please! Don't talk that way! You know—" and Tsirele broke off, her eyes imploring him.

"No is no. How did we all come into this world?"

"Max, do me a favor!"

"Well, from now on I'll watch my tongue. You are a pure maiden and I'm—"

"Don't say anything. Come downstairs with me. There are many things I want to talk over with you."

"We can talk here."

"No, Max, it's not proper for a girl to be with a man in a hotel."

"But we're engaged."

"Especially not with a fiancé."

"Well, I'm not used to these religious formalities. In Paris, life is free. Men and women kiss in the middle of the street."

"Please come down with me!"

"Well, all right."

He put on his hat, realizing that he was not going to persuade Tsirele to stay with him. It was strange, but the very fact that there was absolutely no possibility of remaining with her appealed to his spiteful, devilish side, his inner enemy, and aroused his lust for her. He pressed her to him for the last time. Tsirele pushed him away, becoming flushed and disheveled. Consequently her eyes turned even bluer and more brilliant. A little rabbi in a dress, a little mezuzah. He gave her a last kiss and then went out.

This rabbinical girl had restored his masculine desire. He wanted to take her hand, but she would not permit even that. Max had no idea that such virtue still existed in Poland.

"How much time do you have?" he asked.

"Just an hour or two. We can eat supper together."

Everything was working out. Max had to be at Shkolnikov's at eight. He couldn't take Tsirele to that sorcerer. He stopped a droshky, installed himself next to Tsirele, and asked to be driven to the Lazienki Garden, which he remembered from long ago. Passersby were looking at them and seemed to be surprised. What's the matter? Do they know that she's a rabbi's daughter? Max wondered, realizing that they were looking at her, not him.

He sat silently, thinking that as long as the rabbi wanted him to grow a beard, he had a good couple of weeks' time. By then he would have reached a decision. But what could he accomplish in those few weeks? Send Rochelle a writ of divorce and leave her his whole estate? Bring Tsirele to Argentina and work out some practical solution there? What was the saying? "Let's wait and see how the chips fall." Meanwhile he must enjoy this bright summer day.

He took Tsirele's hand and she no longer pulled it away. He said to her, "God Himself must have sent you to me."

After Max had taken Tsirele home, he vowed he now had only one aim, to free himself from Rochelle and marry Tsirele. He made up his mind not to go to Reyzl Kork anymore and not to meet redheaded Basha on the Sabbath. He had kissed Tsirele in the booth at the restaurant and told her a little about himself, as much as he could. Tsirele spoke of her ideals, confessing that she was not devout even though she was steeped in Jewish observance. She had even read a pamphlet about Darwin, heard a lecturer say that Moses had not performed any miracles on Mount Sinai, and knew who Karl Marx, Kropotkin, and Kautsky were. However, she would never eat pork or light a fire on the Sabbath, not because she believed that God has forbidden it, but out of habit and respect for her parents. Tsirele had her own plans. After the wedding she didn't want to remain living with her parents or even near them. She had no intention of shaving or cutting her hair, wearing a wig, or going to the ritual bathhouse. Tsirele believed in socialism. The revolution would bring an end to exploitation, fanaticism, and war. If she were to have children, she would bring them up in modern fashion, send them to school, make them into useful people, not bench-sitters and parasites. Tsirele said she didn't want to remain in Russia unless there was a new order and the people were given true freedom. What would Max think of moving to Berlin, Paris, or even to London?

"Wherever you want, my dearest," Max replied, "there we will live. Even on the moon . . ." and he kissed her on the forehead, neck, and mouth. One thing he couldn't prevail upon her to do was to go back with him to his hotel.

"You yourself would lose your *derekh erets* for me," she said.

Max hadn't heard that word for respect in a long time. Living abroad, he had forgotten what it meant. It reminded him of Roszkow, *zeyde-bobe* and his teacher Fishele. Despite all her enlightenment, Tsirele's speech had something in it of her father the rabbi. Her words about revolution, the masses, and the proletariat were interspersed with verses from the Pentateuch. She even sang a song to him from the Yiddish theater which ended: "Throw away your aristocratic lineage and be a human being."

In the Lazienki Garden Max had found a restaurant where he ordered potatoes with sour milk. Tsirele wouldn't eat the potatoes because they were cooked in a non-kosher pot, but she drank the coffee and nibbled on a cookie. The two hours passed with extraordinary rapidity. On the way home, the *gumka*, a droshky with rubber wheels, stopped by a store that sold chocolates and Max bought Tsirele a box of candy. He wanted to give her a ten-ruble note but Tsirele wouldn't take it.

"With God's help, after the wedding," she said. Max shuddered. This young girl loved him, was ready to become his wife. Yes, but it was stolen love, built on swindle and villainy.

After they parted, he wrestled with the thought of whether or not he should go to Shkolnikov's séance. He had mentioned Shkolnikov to Tsirele. She had heard of this practitioner of black magic and said people went to him to expose a thief, to recover lost or stolen jewelry, or to identify in a black mirror men who deserted their wives. Tsirele said that as far as she knew, Shkolnikov had yet to do any of these things. It was all superstition, fanaticism, delusion. As for the dead, they are all rotting in their graves and do not come for discussions with anyone.

Max agreed with Tsirele that Shkolnikov probably swindled naïve people out of a few rubles, but he had no place to go this evening. No matter how many girlfriends a man has, or whatever adventures he may embark on, he often finds himself all alone in the evening, unless he has a wife, a home, and children. In what way were Shkolnikov's tricks worse than those in the theater or in cabarets? Besides, the telepathic messages the wizard was sending to Rochelle might indeed help to weaken her magnetism, or whatever it was called.

When he was ready to go, Max hailed a droshky and asked to be taken to Dluga Street. As long as he could do something, he told himself, anything was better than moping about idly. He passed the Iron Gate once more, Przechodnia Street, Bankowy Square (the bank was now closed and a watchman was guarding it outside), Rymarska Street, Tlomackie Street, where the German synagogue with a menorah and a cupola stood. Years ago when Max was living in Warsaw, he had tried to get into this very Christianized Jewish place of worship, but the sexton, dressed in a silk hat, would not let him in. Max had even received a lash from a belt strap for trying to go past the sexton. Now they were surely celebrating a wedding. The electric lights in the menorah were shining. On the square in front of the shul, coaches were waiting. The sound of organ music could be heard from within. Someone still believes in the honesty of women, Max thought wryly. Do we have a choice, ha? Without them the world would go under.

At the bottom of Nalewki and Dluga Streets, Max saw the prison called the Arsenal, its black door and barred windows. A light glimmered inside. For years Max had had a recurrent dream that he was trapped in this very prison. Someone had framed him; it had to do with counterfeit money, a woman, and a murder. In Argentina, after such a dream, he always comforted himself with the thought that, whatever fate had in store for him, he would never be sent back to Warsaw. Now he had come back himself. If he should slip up here, the dream could come true. Max remembered the Polish proverb: *If you're fated to hang, you won't drown.*

The droshky stopped at Bernard Shkolnikov's house and Max alighted. The street seemed poorer and gloomier at night than in the morning. The steps were dark. Max clambered up the stairs, lighting matches. He was assailed by the smell of lard, and something else, oily and rancid. From behind doors, stifled noises could be heard, rumblings, the barking of dogs.

Although he was a man of the underworld, he never got used to Gentiles and their conduct. He loved to eat—Esau's grandchildren are always guzzling—but he had never tasted pork. He had been intimate with *shiksas* but had never loved them. He couldn't even have a decent discussion with Gentiles. He shunned violence and, strange as it may seem, distributed alms to the poor, and in his fashion sought justice. He needed justification for all his sins. Whenever he was threatened by danger, he immediately began to pray to God.

He knocked on Shkolnikov's door but nobody answered. He knocked again, harder. In a while he heard footsteps and the door opened. In the half-dark corridor stood a girl who reminded Max of a sorceress, the kind who roll barrels with the soles of their feet, eat fire, lie down with naked backs on a bed of nails, ride standing on a horse, and dance with a bear. She was enveloped entirely in a black garment that suited her figure perfectly, a combination of coat, pants, stockings, and even shoes. Her hair was cut short in a bob. Through the shadows on her face Max saw a pair of black eyes that shone like a cat's with their own light.

Max was speechless. He began to stammer: "Does the man —how shall I say?—the man who brings back the dead—?"

"Pan Shkolnikov."

"Yes, Shkolnikov."

"What's your name?" the girl asked in Polish.

"Max—Max Barabander."

"Come with me."

The girl moved with silent footsteps, without a rustle. It was as if she slid through the long corridor. After a while she led Max into the same room where he had met Shkolnikov earlier. It was almost dark there. In the half-light Max saw seated and standing figures, men and women. Max was seized by fear and curiosity. I should have taken my revolver, he thought.

Shkolnikov came over to him dressed in a long black garment and shook his hand, saying, "We are waiting for you."

"It's not even eight," Max apologized. He looked around for the girl who had opened the door, but she had disappeared. "This whole hocus-pocus is to get three rubles out of you," Max warned himself. He had the banknote ready in his vest pocket. Someone pointed to a chair next to a small table. Everything was done silently and languidly. People walked about softly, as if in shoes with rubber soles, and gave each other silent signals. There was a trace of the smell of incense that had been lit to dispel bad odors. Even though Max could not hear what people were whispering to each other, he nevertheless picked up snatches of Polish words. "Are they calling up Gentile ghosts?" Max joked to himself. "Even if it's possible, my father and mother wouldn't show up here."

A woman began singing in Polish, in a throaty, rasping voice. The melody reminded Max of the unintelligible bleating of a praying priest. They'll convert me to Christianity yet, Max mused. First one woman sang alone, then others joined her in long, drawn-out tones, wailing as if mourning a death. Max was assailed by a long since forgotten melancholy, the kind which sometimes attacked him in nightmares. The haunted singing was lamenting something for which there is no comfort. "Such singing really could summon the dead from their graves," Max said to himself. Did he imagine he heard Arturo's name? They were chanting a Christian *al mole rakhmim*, "God Have Mercy," for his dead son. How do they know about Arturo? Max wondered, having forgotten he had told Shkolnikov about his son. Everything in Max became still, taut. Again he remembered a word that had long since gone out of his mind, *klepsydra*? What is *klepsydra*? Where was that word used—in Spanish? He had come to mock, but now he felt like weeping. Suddenly the girl who had opened the door for him appeared. She was wearing the same outfit except that over her shoulders hung a black shawl. She sat down at a table and everyone placed their fingers on the edge. A woman took Max's hands and put them there. "*Lekko*—lightly," she whispered to him. Max had heard about people who asked questions at a table; it even had a name in Roszkow—*teshele*. His father had spoken of the wonders that a table can perform if put together with wooden pegs instead of nails. The rabbi of Roszkow said it was forbidden to get involved with such things because it was sorcery. Now Max himself was experiencing it. The singing stopped and a leaden stillness followed.

Max couldn't believe it, but the table began to vibrate and rock as if it were no longer an inanimate object and had acquired a living force. Was someone lifting it? All the hands were on top of the table, not under it. How could the table be trembling and fluttering under his fingers? From time to time the table rose, as if it were ready to take flight. What kind of black magic were they performing? They asked the table questions and the table answered—one knock for yes, two for no. How could this little table know whether the fat woman's husband would return from America? "It's all delusion and illusion!" Max said to himself. Shkolnikov then asked Max if he wanted to ask something.

"Will Rochelle divorce me?"

The little table answered: "Yes."

"Will Tsirele become my wife?"

The table seemed to hesitate for a while. Then it knocked twice: "No."

"Is my father alive?"

"No."

"My mother?"

The table didn't respond at all.

Max didn't know what to ask anymore. Both his parents had died, one shortly after the other. Why would the table answer the question about his father and not his mother? The others hastened to ask their questions. Max became tired of holding his hands on the table and moved his chair back.

When the little table was taken away, the girl began to speak in a voice that did not seem at all related to her slender figure. The odd sound that issued from her was neither that of a woman nor that of a man, but a mixture of both. She spoke an aristocratic Polish that Max barely understood. She was speaking about someone, called out a name that sounded strange, relayed messages from the dead. The spirits she summoned gave signs, recalled places and dates, reported all that had transpired with them since they left the earth. Suddenly there was whispering. Something appeared in the dark which looked like a glove or a plaster hand. Someone put a bowl or a pot on the floor. The hand slowly floated in the air and swam over to the pot and sank in. Then it rose up again and moved in the opposite direction. Max was entranced. Whose hand was it? How was it suspended in midair? He strained his eyes but could see nothing more than the hand. He heard a whispering and a suppressed sighing. Something miraculous had happened before his eyes. Was he dreaming? He wanted to ask one of the seated figures what was going on, but before he could utter a word, someone nudged his arm, a sign he should keep quiet. Other miracles took place. A little trumpet appeared out of nowhere and began to emit a sound like a ram's horn, on one note, in wailing tones. Although it was dark, the trumpet shone as if from its own light. A mandolin strummed.

Suddenly a voice called out: "Arturo is here. He wants to talk to you . . ."

Later, Max himself was unable to recall how it all transpired. In an instant his face became wet, as if someone had poured tepid water over him. A figure floated up. He heard a voice. Arturo spoke to him in Polish, but in his excitement Max forgot that Arturo's language was Spanish. He heard Arturo pleading:

"Papa, I miss you . . . Papa, I'm not dead. I'm alive. I'm here next to you . . . Papa, I know everything you went through. I met *zeyde-bobe* here and we prayed together for you . . . I'm still your loyal son . . . and I miss you. We talk about you all the time . . . You don't have to grieve over me. I'm happy where I am. Mother will soon be with us here, but you still have important things to do on Planet Earth. Remember, Papa, I'm with you. Do everything that Pan Shkolnikov tells you to. He is loved by us. He brings us in contact with our dear ones. Forgive me, Papa, but I must go. But I will return. I have greetings for you from our entire family."

The figure vanished. "It's Arturo, Arturo!" something in Max cried. "God in heaven, I talked with my son. If Rochelle only knew about this!" Max had not cried at Arturo's funeral, but now his face was wet with tears. His eyes burned and wept of their own accord.

Max no longer took stock of what was happening. A drunkenness possessed him. He stood, his legs became limp, he slept. When he touched a chair and sat down, it was as if he fell into the seat. His strength left him, and even though he did not pass out, he was aware that he felt faint. Sparks ignited before his eyes, hovered, rose and fell. His ears felt as if they were deafened. He heard words but couldn't make sense of them. He had a feeling that his chair was falling and he with it, sinking into muck or an abyss. "Is this my end?" Max asked himself.

A light began to shine as if some force had heard his thoughts and tried to cheer him up. It was a red light, the kind sometimes used to prevent blindness when a child had the measles. Max discerned a few faces including the girl, the sorceress, who was sitting on a chair leaning back, with two men holding her by the wrists. And once again there was murmuring and moaning. The spirit, or whatever it was floating in the dark, had dipped its hand into paraffin and left an impression. The woman carried the bowl or pot around, and everyone took a look. Could this be Arturo's hand? Max took out a handkerchief and wiped his face, completely bathed in sweat. His shirt was wet. The two men who were holding the girl's wrists now let them go. She had her head thrown back, her eyes closed, looking as if she was sunk in a deep sleep. They tried to wake her and she cried in her sleep, groaned, shuddered.

Cool beads of perspiration ran down Max's spine. He sat there soaked, weakened, hollow, and perplexed by his own condition. "If only Rochelle were here!" an inner voice cried. He wanted to divorce her, but he would have liked to share with her the satisfaction he had experienced this evening. He had seen Arturo, heard his voice. Three rubles are not enough, Max decided. I'll give him ten. Max put his hand in his vest pocket and touched a damp banknote. He had perspired through his shirt and even through the lining of his vest. Max heard Shkolnikov trying to revive the medium.

"Wake up, Theresa, wake up . . . Theresa!"

She gave a last shudder and woke up. Her black eyes looked frightened. A woman embraced her, kissed her. Someone came in with a kerosene lamp and a cup of tea or coffee. In the light he saw the little table, the pot of paraffin, and those that had gathered here. In the darkness it had seemed that the house was full of people, but he counted only five women and three men. Were the others ghosts or spirits of the dead? He had come here a skeptic, but his doubts had vanished. He had witnessed a miracle. The dead revealed themselves to the living, talked to them. He had seen Arturo's figure, heard his voice . . .

Max called Shkolnikov over to a corner and gave him ten rubles. Shkolnikov, not even looking at the note, put it right in his pocket. Max wanted to approach the girl Theresa, but she had disappeared.

"Is that your sister?" Max asked, and Shkolnikov mumbled, "Yes, my sister."

"Can I talk to her?"

"Not today. The séance weakens her. She is more dead than alive."

The assembled people began to depart. They left as if from a holy place, without any leave-taking, in the same way that people would go home from the shul in Roszkow on Yom Kippur after the Kol Nidre service. Max became aware that no one was left but him and Shkolnikov. Standing by the draped window in a long coat, small, dark, and with black eyes half covered by disheveled eyebrows, Shkolnikov looked at him with a frozen glance, like a sorcerer. Max was struck with terror. He realized that he would have to go down three floors by way of the dark, long, and crooked stairs.

"Was that my son?" he asked, and Shkolnikov nodded his head.

"Arturo spoke Spanish, not Polish."

"They speak the language of the medium. They make use of her tongue, her organs."

"Will it help me?"

"Yes, in time."

"When shall I come here again?"

"Monday. No, Tuesday."

"How do you get out of here?" Max asked.

"Come, I'll take you down."

"I'd like to say a few words to your sister."

"Not today."

Shkolnikov led him through the long corridor. He stood by the open door and Max went down the stairs with slow steps and with the clumsiness of a person who has almost forgotten how to walk after a long illness. His knees buckled under him. The steps seemed to him to be too high, too far from each other. He held on to the railing like an old man. When he got outside, he felt a cool breeze blowing. Dluga Street stretched out before him in semidarkness with a middle-of-the-night emptiness. No trolley ran by, no droshky passed; he was walking all alone on an empty sidewalk, altered and shaken, like someone who has left a hospital or a prison where he has been incarcerated for years.

For a moment Max didn't remember where he was and what he was doing. He stopped and then he remembered. Yes, he was here in Warsaw. he was staying at the Hotel Bristol. He had become entangled with Tsirele, the rabbi's daughter, and with Reyzl Kork, Shmuel Smetena's girlfriend. But how was he going to get from here to the hotel? Max waited till someone passed by, and asked. A man showed him the way. Where Kozia Street met Podwale Street there was a feeling of backstreet danger. I'll get killed here yet! Max thought. The widely spaced gas lamps shed little light. From the ancient houses humming and rustling sounds could be heard. Cool winds blew in from the Vistula. Max halted once again. Why should Arturo, who was buried in Buenos Aires, appear before him in an apartment in Warsaw? When had he learned to speak Polish? It was all a swindle, a swindle. A streetwalker accosted him.

"Shall we go?"

"No, girlie," and Max gave her ten groschen.

he rabbi had invited him to eat at his home for the Sabbath, so Max bought all sorts of delicacies for the family—kosher wine, rabbinically certified kosher lox, a bottle of the sweet liqueur women like to sip after dinner, a box of chocolates for Tsirele (also certified kosher), and a bouquet. He arrived two hours before candle-lighting. The people on Krochmalna Street stared at Max in astonishment as he climbed out of the droshky with his packages and his flowers. As he walked up the steps, from every door he was assailed by smells of fish, onions, parsley, and freshly baked yeast cakes. When he went into the rabbi's house the rebbetzin, disheveled and flushed, looked at him in amazement. Clapping her hands, she called out: "Tsirele, come look!"

Tsirele was in the midst of tying up the *cholent*, the Sabbath stew, with a strip of ribbon ripped from an old shirt. On the paper covering the *cholent* pot she had inked the number of their house and apartment. She shouted: "Mama, see how much he's brought!"

"Really, we don't need all of this. On Purim, with God's help, you can send gifts," the rebbetzin protested.

"That's a long way off," said Max.

"What is this, kosher lox?" she said. "Who eats lox? And what do we need liqueur for? Nobody here drinks. And flowers ... what do you do with flowers?"

"I'll put them in water so that they will remain fresh," Tsirele replied.

"That's a Gentile fashion. Jews don't keep flowers."

"Flowers are also not kosher?"

"No, but it's throwing away money."

"What's this?" Tsirele cried. "Oh, a box of chocolates! Just look at the box! It must have cost at least two rubles."

"Tsirele, it's for you!"

"Many thanks, but what a spendthrift you are!"

Tsirele went to attend to the *cholent*, which had to be taken to the bakery right away. Max asked for the rabbi but he had not yet come back from the ritual bath. From the kitchen emanated a mixture of smells—fish, chicken soup, carrot tsimmes, and wine that the rebbetzin had distilled from raisins. Max went into the prayer room, where the congregation prayed on Sabbath mornings. There was a table set with candlesticks—two silver and four brass—two challahs covered with an embroidered cloth, a challah knife with a mother-of-pearl handle, and a decanter with an old and dented *kiddush* cup. All was in readiness for the Sabbath.

Max, pacing back and forth, took a holy book out of the bookcase and soon put it back. He came closer to the Holy Ark, parted the curtain, and opened the door a crack. One Torah scroll covered with a maroon mantle was leaning by itself, and over it hung a breastplate and a pointer. The odor within the ark was a mixture of citron, wax, and something else that was undefinable.

Max knew full well that he should not have opened the Holy Ark, or touched such a consecrated place at all. Only yesterday he had made his hands unclean by laying them on the séance table that performed magic. Now it felt good to stand there surrounded by sacred books. His soul was refreshed by the sanctity breathed upon him. How fortunate the rabbi is, Max thought. His path is a straight one . . . He's happy in this world and he'll have Paradise in the next.

He went out on the balcony, feeling that he belonged here. In every nook and cranny of the street preparations were being made for the Sabbath. The bakers were not carrying rolls but challah, *shtritsl* (white bread loaves), and cakes. Men were coming back from the ritual bath, as their red faces, damp beards and sidelocks revealed. Here and there the half doors of stores were being shut. Through open windows you could see men or women setting candles firmly in molten wax and girls carrying *cholent* to the bakeries.

Max looked at No. 15 and recognized Esther, the baker's wife; their encounter had ended so disastrously. She was sitting on a bench by the gate, weighing a huge twisted challah on a scale. All over the square, which usually swarmed with thieves and loose women, there hovered a Sabbath-eve peacefulness.

Max had almost forgotten about the Sabbath in Argentina. On Saturdays Rochelle and her maid would always iron laundry in the patio. While the women were ironing, Arturo and Max played billiards. But in Warsaw, the Sabbath was observed strictly as a holy day.

When Max heard the rabbi's voice, he went out to greet him. The rabbi's beard was damp. He had already taken his satin coat and fur-edged hat out of the clothes closet. He nodded to Max, but seemed too preoccupied to talk.

The rebbetzin ran in, her wig disheveled. "God forbid, today I'll yet desecrate the Sabbath."

"There's still a half hour left until sundown," the rabbi comforted her.

"Woe is me! It's already time to light the candles!" And the rebbetzin ran out again.

Max went to pray in the Neustadter prayerhouse with the rabbi, Itchele, and Moyshele. From under Itchele's little velvet cap two sidelocks protruded, red as fire. Moyshele, a small child of six, had blond sidelocks and big blue eyes. Both children carried little prayer books. Max had brought them candy and nuts. They already knew that "the dandy" would become Tsirele's fiancé. They looked at him with curiosity, suspicion, and dubious affection.

In the Neustadter prayerhouse the candles and the gas lamps were already burning. The Hasidim were milling about in satin coats, with fur-edged hats on their heads, reciting the Song of Songs. Seeing that the rabbi had brought a modern Jew with him, they came toward him to extend their greetings.

The first greeter was Reb Getsl, a narrow-faced man with a sparse white beard and scraggly white sidelocks, wearing a long satin coat and shoes and stockings of the Orthodox. "Where are you from?" he asked.

Straightaway Max began to choke up. "From Buenos Aires in Argentina."

"What kind of country is that?"

"It's in America."

"New York?"

"No, from Buenos Aires to New York is as far as from Buenos Aires to Warsaw."

The men shrugged their shoulders.

Reb Getsl asked, "What are you doing here?"

"Came to visit relatives."

"To the rabbi?"

"My relatives are in Roszkow."

"*Nu* . . ."

The congregants returned to the Song of Songs. Soon one of the Hasidim went up to the pulpit for the prayer "Give thanks."

It all seemed extraordinarily strange to Max and extraordinarily familiar. He recognized the melody and the words even though he did not understand their meaning: "*Yorday hayom booniyoys oysay milokho bimayim rabim* (They that go down to the sea in ships do their work in vast waters) . . . *vayitsaku el hashem batsar lohem umimtsukoysayhem* (and they cried out to God in their anguish and he rescued them from their woes)." After that they said *lekhu neraneno* (Let us sing in praise of the Lord), and the prayer leader sang *lekho doydi* (Let us go, my love, toward the bride). When they recited the stanza *boi besholem* (Come in peace), everyone turned to the western wall.

After praying, the men came over to Max and wished him a good Sabbath. See, I'm not a stranger here! Max thought with astonishment. In all the years he had felt like a stranger everywhere, no matter whether it was in a hotel, a summerhouse, a theater, a casino. At home on Rosh Hashanah and Yom Kippur he had bought a ticket to the local synagogue, but nobody knew him. It was a cold, non-Hasidic synagogue, where the children were already using Spanish to scream at each other. Once in

Buenos Aires he had come upon a Sephardic synagogue, where
people were talking Ladino, and suddenly he was once again in
a prayerhouse like the one in Roszkow.

Here in Warsaw Jews came over to greet him, to question
him as to where he was from, what he did. The beadle came
over and asked, "What's your name?"

"Max. I mean, Mordkhe."

"What was your father called?"

"Abraham Nathan."

"What are you, a Kohen, a Levite, or an Israelite?"

Max stood there perplexed. He remembered these words
but had forgotten their significance.

The beadle asked, "Did your father perform the priestly
benediction?"

"The benediction? No."

"Did he wash the hands of the *kohanim*?"

"Wash their hands? No."

"In that case you are an Israelite. We'll call you up to the
Torah tomorrow."

Max stammered a few words. "I don't remember the benediction."

"Oh? The rabbi will show you where it is in the prayer
book," and the beadle turned from him and shrugged.

"You don't have to be ashamed, Mordkhe," Tsirele's father
said. "A Jew can always repent. 'He repented and he was healed,'
so said the prophet. That's why we were given choice, so that
we could repent. Even in the netherworld, repentance prevails."

"Argentina is a Christian country."

"God is everywhere."

How different the apartment looked when Max returned
with the rabbi and his sons: candles were burning, the rooms

looked clean and tidy. The rebbetzin and Tsirele were wearing their Sabbath clothes, the rebbetzin in her Sabbath wig and a long dress decorated with arabesques, Tsirele in a white blouse and a narrow black skirt.

The rabbi sang *sholem aleykhem* and the prayer *eyshes khayel* ("Woman of Valor"). He pronounced the sabbath *kiddush* and gave Max some of the raisin wine to drink. Max said a blessing, just like the others, over the poppy-seed-covered challah. Everything—the gefilte fish, the chicken soup with rice, the meat, the carrot tsimmes—had a homemade flavor. Between servings, the rabbi sang Sabbath songs and both boys joined in.

Mother and daughter sat at the end of the table. Tsirele kept glancing at Max. At times she smiled, at times she looked serious, now and then she winked at him and nodded her head.

The rebbetzin looked at him severely, critically, angrily. The rabbi began to say *thou* to Max, but the rebbetzin continued to use the polite form. After saying grace, the rabbi started to question Max about distant lands. Was there a rabbi in Buenos Aires? Did he wear a beard and sidelocks? *Nu*, and what about in London? And in Paris? Are there studyhouses, Hasidic prayerhouses, yeshivas? Max didn't really know what to say, but he remembered that there was a yeshiva in New York.

The rabbi stroked his beard. "The Kotsker rabbi said: 'The Torah wanders . . .' "

"Is there a ritual bath in Buenos Aires?" the rebbetzin asked.

"Ha, I don't know."

"In that case, all the children are bastards."

The rabbi deliberated. "Even a son born of a woman who is not ritually clean is not a bastard. There probably is a ritual bath there. Wherever there are Jews, there is a ritual bath."

"Yes, Rabbi, there must be."

"I wouldn't send my daughter there for all the riches in the world," said the rebbetzin.

"We'll come and live here."

"A Jewish girl must keep all the laws of family purity."

"Whatever she wants, we will do. Your daughter is holy to me."

The rabbi proposed to Max that he stay over at his house. "It's a long way to the Hotel Bristol. Who knows if you are allowed to carry things? Very often the wires connecting the *Eyrev*—which marks the boundaries within which articles may be carried on the Sabbath—are severed."

"What will I be carrying, then?"

"You'll have to bring your tallis." Max felt a bitter taste in his mouth . . .

The rebbetzin gave her mocking smile. "He surely doesn't have a tallis."

The rabbi seemed frightened. "You don't have a tallis and tefillin?"

"When I go into a shul, they lend them to me," said Max, justifying himself with a lie, quite surprised at how easily he extricated himself from the trap.

The rabbi pushed the *kiddush* cup away.

"That's what happens when you move away from Jewish-ness," he said half to himself, half to Max. "It is said: 'If you leave the Torah for one day, it abandons you for two.' What do we have other than the Torah? Without the Torah, we are all, God forbid, lost. If with God's help, you become my son-in-law, you will have to be a Jew . . ."

"Rabbi, I will do everything you tell me, even if you tell me to jump into the fire!"

"God forbid! A Jew may sacrifice his life, heaven forbid, only if he is forced to take part in idolatry, murder, or sexual immorality. The Torah is a Torah of life. The Gemara says: 'You shall live by the words of the Torah, not die by them.' One has to live with this commandment. The Torah is the source of life."

"Yes, Holy Rabbi."

"Father, don't lecture him so much. He's a Jew, not a Gentile," Tsirele cried. The rabbi gave his daughter a look.

"There are some things one must not forget," he said.

On the Sabbath, after the *cholent*, Max said goodbye to the rabbi and started walking toward Ciepla Street. Even though Tsirele had hinted that she would be able to steal away for an hour or two, Max said that he had to meet a relative. At three o'clock he was to meet Basha, the girl Reyzl had introduced him to.

It was a quarter past two when he left the rabbi's house. The street smelled of *cholent*, potato pudding, and onions with fat. All the pious men and women were napping after the meal, but the young people, the men in short clothes arm in arm with "modern" girls, were out strolling. It reminded Max of the eve of Rosh Hashanah at Roszkow, when people walked to the lake to cast off their sins.

Dandies in hats and suits that looked brand-new, with stiff collars and dickeys, polished shoes and colored ties were carrying canes on the Sabbath. As for the women, a new style had come into fashion: dresses so narrow that they were forced to take short, mincing steps. Even though it was summer, a number of the elegant ladies of Krochmalna Street draped fur pieces over their shoulders. Women's hats were decorated with wooden cherries, plums, grapes, even ostrich feathers. Here and there Max noticed a girl who had padded her seat and plumped up each breast with a little pillow.

The stores were all shut tight, but Max remembered that there were *tchaynes*, little teahouses, open on the Sabbath. You could also buy sweets in a confectionary and beer in a tavern —all on credit. Just as soon as you left Krochmalna Street, Gnoyna Street, and other such streets where "God's Cossacks," the society that guarded the Sabbath, had their spies, you could do whatever your heart desired. Some couples went to the Yiddish theater, others to the Illusion, where moving pictures were shown, or to the Saxony Gardens.

Max had lots of time until three o'clock and he walked slowly, observing everyone. Some young men were wearing derbies, others straw hats. Occasionally someone appeared wearing a broad-brimmed felt hat over long hair, a cape over his shoulders, and a bow instead of a tie at his neck. This was the fashion for the socialists, the intelligentsia, those who read books, went to concerts or meetings, and conducted discussions on how to better mankind. Max also recognized pimps and whores, more dressed up than the others, and in brighter colors. They laughed loudly, cracked pumpkin seeds, draped masses of fake jewelry over themselves, and left scented trails of cheap perfume. On the doorsteps sat women nursing their babies and gossiping.

Between Ciepla and Krochmalna Streets there was a military barracks where the Woliner Regiment was housed. Left of Ciepla Street, where Max was supposed to meet Basha, was a policemen's barracks, before which a guard stood near a sentry box. In the large courtyard a noncommissioned officer was drilling soldiers. Children stopped to watch them and the soldiers chased them away. The soldiers were learning how to stab a straw dummy, running at it with bayonets extended, piercing its straw guts.

It was ten past three and Basha had still not shown up. Had she forgotten or perhaps changed her mind? Max looked around on all sides. It had come to such a pass that he was unable to remain by himself for any length of time. There wasn't even a Jewish newspaper for him to read on the Sabbath.

Max had read the Friday paper from beginning to end, even the jokes and the serialized novel without knowing how it began. The story was set in Petersburg and had something to do with a veiled lady, a murderous baron, and a young orphan girl who had come from the provinces to the big city. Max often wondered where these writers got their material. Were they writing about their own lives, or were they simply adept at invention? The suspense in this novel had already drawn him in. He was looking forward to the next installment to learn who Olga was and why she had covered her face with heavy veils.

"Well, that scullery maid stood me up," he said to himself. "So what do I do now? Go somewhere to a moving picture? Go for a ride by myself to the gardens?" His watch showed it was already twenty-five minutes past three. I'll just stay here five more minutes! Max decided. You don't wait more than a half hour even for the Countess Potocki, not to speak of a cook from Krochmalna Street.

Inwardly cursing Basha, Max imagined himself the Governor-General of Poland, ordering her to the women's section of Powiak prison. Why not hang her? Let her know that Max Barabander is not someone you can make a fool of. "I'll just go back to Tsirele. If she's sitting on the balcony, I'll signal her to come down."

Max shook his head over the state he was in. Everybody

else had somehow settled down and found his mate. He, Max, with a whole slew of women, was still all alone. How was it possible? It was either a curse or—what had Shkolnikov called it?—hypnotism. Rochelle had cast a spell on him, with her telepathic messages. Maybe she had sent one to Basha not to come to their rendezvous.

At that moment Max lifted his eyes and saw Basha coming toward him from Krochmalna Street. She was wearing a yellow dress and a hat with flowers over her red hair. She looked poor, provincial, and a little bit frightened. Max ran toward her: "Bashale!"

The girl said breathlessly, "Are you still here? I thought you would be gone by now!"

"Why did you come so late?"

The girl made a sign that she had to catch her breath.

"They never send me out for tea on the Sabbath. The old man doesn't drink Sabbath tea because he says they cook on the Sabbath in who knows what. Today he had a brainstorm and wanted tea. What could I do? I went off for tea to Shmuel Malakh, whose tea is strictly kosher. I get there and there's a big crowd. By the time they boiled the water and I got everything to the table and got dressed, it was a quarter past three. I began to run so fast I almost broke a leg. I'm not used to high heels. What will the man think? I wonder. I almost had a fit. Thank God you're here. A thousand apologies. When you are someone's servant you must do what they tell you. Otherwise they send you away and don't even pay you for the season."

"I understand, I understand. Don't take it to heart. If you do as I say, you'll be a lady, not a servant for some good-for-nothing."

"The old lady began asking me where I was going and why

I'm all dressed up. She bedecks herself with all kinds of cheap trinkets and she begrudges me washing my face."

"She begrudges you because you are pretty and she is ugly."

"How did you know that? She's round as a barrel. Every summer she goes to Falenicz and comes back weighing thirty pounds more. This summer they're going to Ciechocinek, but that's three weeks away."

"You'll stay home?"

"What else? Do you think they'd take me with them?"

"I'll come to you."

Basha thought for a while. "Let's go on Grzybowska Street. Krochmalna Street is too much like a small town. Soon they'll start gossiping about us."

"We'll take a droshky."

"On the Sabbath? No."

"If you want to go to Argentina, you can't be so pious."

"That's another story . . ."

It was strange to think that he was depending on a girl like this, but he realized if she hadn't come today, he would have felt lost. He walked her to Grzybowska Street, and then to Krolewska.

"Where are we going?" Basha asked.

"You're not hungry, are you?"

"Hungry? After the *cholent?*"

"Perhaps you want to have some coffee?"

"Coffee on the Sabbath? I just ate meat."

What kind of dolt is this? Max wondered. Wants to go to Argentina to become a whore and is afraid to eat dairy after meat. She surely doesn't understand what Reyzl Kork wants of her. She's a kosher little fool.

"Come over to my place," he said. "We'll talk things over."

"Where do you live?"

"In the Hotel Bristol."

Basha was silent for a long time. "You think they'll let me in?"

"If you come with me, you'll be my guest."

"What will we do there?"

"We'll talk like two friends."

"Well, all right," said Basha after some hesitation.

Max himself didn't know why he asked her to come to the hotel. He usually didn't like redheaded women, especially freckled ones. But he had no desire to go to a garden or a theater. He took her by the arm and she nestled close to him.

At the entrance of the Hotel Bristol Basha became frightened and clung to him. He took her upstairs and into his room.

Basha looked around, shaking her head. "This is the first time in my life that I've been in a hotel."

"What's a hotel? Rooms like all rooms. It just costs more. Take off your hat, make yourself at home."

"But where does a dog have a home?"

"Well now, Basha!"

She took off her hat and her red hair cascaded down. As her hairpins fell out, Max gathered them up. Basha sat down and said, "Some people in this world have a good life. My cousin went away to America. He was a shoemaker's apprentice and his pay was water for his groats. There he became—what's it called—a manufacturer. He sent a photograph and his own mother didn't recognize him. He had a top hat on his head like a chimney. His wife speaks only *Engalish*. A real squire. Here he was called Shmerl, there he named himself Sam. When my father read the letter, everybody in the house began to cry like it was Yom Kippur."

"Why did they cry?"

"For joy."

"Yes, it's true. Here it's a tortured life. In America you can work your way up. The main thing is not to be fanatical. Why can't you eat dairy after meat? It's all nonsense."

"That's what my mother taught me."

"In your stomach everything gets mixed up—meat, milk, even a piece of pork."

"Do you eat pork?"

"No, but not because you're not supposed to. I just don't like it. We'll go down later and have some coffee. There's a café. Let's stay here till half past seven."

"What are you talking about? I have to prepare the last meal of the Sabbath."

"Can't they help themselves?"

"The old woman would get rid of me right away."

"If she sends you away, come to me. You'll travel with me and I'll take care of you. Come here!"

Max went over to her and took her by the wrists. She gave a start but did not pull away. He lifted her up and kissed her on the lips. Flustered, she gazed at him with her green eyes. He kissed her again and she kissed him back. He embraced her and pressed her breasts against his chest. She murmured, "What are you doing? Someone could come in."

"Nobody will come in."

He felt desire for her and tried to undress her, but she caught his hands.

"Not now."

"When?"

"We must be friends first."

"Tell me the truth, have you had someone?"

"Nobody. May God punish me!"

Max knew that soon he could do whatever he wanted with her. Lately he had had so many failures with women that he was afraid to push his luck. At one moment he was overcome with lust, and the next moment it receded. It was as if something within him, an inner enemy, was teasing him and trying to embarrass him. He gave her a long kiss and she returned it, biting his mouth. Someone knocked at the door and Basha wrestled herself loose and began to fix her hair.

Max opened the door and a maid in a white apron with a cap over her hair said, "You're wanted on the telephone."

He recognized Reyzl Kork's voice. "Max, is that you?" she said. "I didn't expect you to be in the hotel but I tried. Did you meet Basha?"

"Yes, she's with me in the hotel."

"Well, *mazel tov*."

"It's not what you think."

"What are you doing with her, reciting psalms?"

"We're talking."

"She'll have to be corrupted, but not too quickly. Max, Shmuel left this morning for Lodz."

"He rides on the Sabbath?"

"It's better to ride on the Sabbath than in the middle of the week. The train is empty."

"I see . . ."

"You can't keep Basha there too long. I know her master and mistress. If they don't get their fish and sour milk for the last meal of the Sabbath, they think the world is coming to an end. What are you doing Sabbath evening?"

"I'll recite the Havdalah prayer and sing *hamavdil*."

"Come over and we'll sing together."

"It's a deal."

"What time will you be here?"

"Seven o'clock."

"Don't come to me with a full stomach. If you come here, you have to eat."

"I'll eat your bones."

"If you can, then you may."

Max hung up the receiver and returned to Basha. He had feared he would be alone this evening, but some demon was watching over him. Only everything was parceled out bit by bit, keeping him in suspense.

Basha was holding a comb and fixing her red hair with it.

"The old man where I work has a telephone," she said. "In the middle of the night it starts to ring and wakes us all up. The old man answers the phone and someone says, 'The strings to your drawers are trailing.' "

"A joker, eh?"

"These pranksters get everyone into hot water. They call up a young wife and say her husband is carrying on with all kinds of Gentile women and start them fighting. Or they tell the man that his wife has a lover. They call up a rabbi, a general, whoever they can think of. My old people stopped answering the phone in the middle of the night; they let it ring till it stops."

"Can I call you on the telephone?"

"If the old people aren't at home, yes. Once someone called from my hometown. The old man began asking him who he was, what he wanted, and cross-examined him so long that he hung up."

"The old man is probably jealous of you. Does he touch you?"

"No more than a pinch on the backside. That's all he can get out of me."

"And he's a Hasid, hm?"

"Goes to the synagogue every morning. On the Sabbath, when he sings hymns, he can make you deaf."

"Well, the man is a pig," Max said to himself. He still felt the taste of Basha's kisses on his lips. Despite the fact that he had been involved with the female sex over the years, he realized once again that you could never really understand how their minds work. They were all the same, yet they were all different. Seemingly they did everything according to reason, but their way of thinking was enigmatic. Why, for instance, did she kiss him? Was it because he had promised to take her abroad, or did she like him? Reyzl Kork's words, that Basha had to be corrupted but not too quickly, excited and frightened him. "What kind of a corrupter am I? I myself am corrupted."

Max dreaded meeting with Reyzl. She had spoken openly. "Shmuel left" . . . In her voice there had been a wicked little laugh. He said to Basha, "If you won't sleep with me, let's go out and walk to a restaurant."

"I can't walk. These heels are killing me."

"If that's the case, we'll eat something here."

"God forbid if I'm hungry."

"What do you want to do?"

"I wish I could sit here a hundred years."

Max laughed: "And you wouldn't sleep with me at night?"

"I probably would."

"Tell me something about yourself. When did you start as a servant girl?"

"Oh, when I was nine years old. First I was a servant for a rich man in Wyszkow, Reb Nosele Yavrover. But he had

another servant and I used to help her. She didn't let me near
the kitchen, but if the milk boiled over it was my fault. She used
to call me the red heifer because I have red hair. People think
men are bad, but when a woman is wicked she's worse than a
thousand men. She had a lover, a butcher boy, and when he
used to come to her on the Sabbath, after the *cholent*, she was
sweet as sugar. His name was Shloyme, but she called him
Lyame. 'Lyame, go here; Lyame, go there.' He used to look at
me and pull my braids. That would make her sick and she would
have a fit. Once my boss lost ten rubles and she said I took
them, calling me a thief. My grandmother used to say, 'God
takes long and punishes hard.' God punished her because
Lyame was called up for military service. The rich maim themselves or bribe the doctor, but a butcher boy doesn't have any
money. He was strong as an ox. At his swearing-in, Royze-Leah,
as she was called, ran after him and cried as if it were a funeral.
He looked back and shouted, 'What are you wailing for? I'm
not dead yet!' Months passed and she didn't get a letter. Every
day she went to the post office to inquire about a letter and the
Gentiles laughed at her. A half year later a letter came, not from
him, but from Royze-Leah's cousin. Lyame had run away from
the soldiers and gone off to America. When Royze heard the
news—her boss read the letter to her—she began to cry and
couldn't stop. She ran up and down, slapping her hands together
and screaming, 'Lyame, what have you done to me? Lyame, why
did you shame me?' At first they let her cry. But when one day
passed and then another and she did nothing in the house, the
mistress sent her away."

"And you took her place?"

"The mistress didn't trust me in the kitchen. They dis-
missed me."

"What happened to Royze-Leah?"

"Before she was fat as a pig. After that letter, her flesh fell away from her as if she was wasting away from consumption. I went to Warsaw, but when I came back for Passover, she had left for America."

"She took Lyame away from his American wife?"

"You're a clever one! How did you guess? That's what she tried to do, but she was out of luck. In America when you get married, it's all over; there the women are the top of the heap."

"What happened to Royze?"

"What happened after that I don't know. People go away and they don't write. My mother used to say, 'Over the water is like being in the next world.' "

"You really believe that God punished her?"

Basha was silent for a long time. "Who would punish if not God?" she said.

"It could be that God sits in the seventh heaven and worries as much about this world as he does over last year's snow."

"No, that can't be."

"Why not?"

"Just because. There was a religious man where we lived, Reb Todrus, and he said, 'God is our father and we are His children. He looks down from the sky and sees every little thing. If a person gets a little splinter under his nail, God knows it.' "

"Why does he let a splinter get under the nail?"

"For a sin."

"Why is Stolypin a minister and your father a poor school-teacher?"

"Who is this Stolypin? They gorge themselves in this world, and when they get to the other world they are dragged down to hell. There they have to lie on a bed of nails."

"In that case, you'll be punished because you kissed me."

"What? Yes, maybe."

"Still, you did kiss me. If you go with me to Argentina, you won't be a rebbetzin there, I'm telling you beforehand."

"Yes, I know."

"And despite that you want to go?"

"I can't stand it here anymore. The years pass and you get old. Without a dowry a girl can't get a man. The old woman eats me up like a worm and there's nothing to wake up for. It's washing the dishes again, making the fire again, peeling the potatoes again. Thursday and Friday I work like a horse. The Sabbath comes and I sit by the window and look out at the trash bin."

"You'd rather be in hell than lead such a life?"

"It's a long way to hell . . ."

"The books say there's no hell."

"Oh? If so, then that's really good . . ."

"Well, come. Let's go."

Max got up. Basha got up, too. He took her by the shoulders, bent down and kissed her. All his fears left him. He kissed her harder and harder, pulling her toward the bed. She tore herself away from him. "Don't do this. I'm a decent girl!"

"You've been decent long enough!" He threw her down on the bed. Basha's face became inflamed. Her eyes turned intensely green. A mixture of anger and love showed on her face. She struggled with him, catching him by the hands with an unbelievable strength. Through all this wrestling she somehow managed to smile.

"Please! Have pity. Not today!"

"When?"

"Another time," she panted.

He tried to take her by force, ripping her dress.

"You're tearing my dress!" she hissed. Suddenly he felt her nails on his face. She scratched him like a cat, without anger or hate. He felt the warmth of blood. He let her go and she jumped up with a swiftness and agility that astonished him.

"Oh, Mama, blood!" she cried. And she began to kiss him, embracing him, licking him. She ran over to the sink, wet a handkerchief, and pressed it to his face. He wiped himself.

"You wild animal," he cried. "When?"

"Another time," she answered. "Not in the middle of the day." And she burst out crying. In an instant her face changed, revealing a mixture of fear, devotion, and regret. She hovered over him like a mother who has scolded her child. Once again she ran over to wet the handkerchief at the faucet.

"Do you have any iodine?" she asked. And she let loose a piercing howl like a little girl who has been done a terrible injury. She hung on him, wept on his chest, kissed his shirt, made up with him. He went over to the mirror and Basha trailed after him. He saw two scratches, one on his forehead and one on his left cheek.

How will I show myself to Reyzl Kork? he thought. And later in front of Tsirele? It will take a week for this to heal.

Max was angry with this provincial girl who had stood up to him. But she had aroused his lust and he still desired her. He caught her by the hair.

"It's now or never!"

"*Tatele*, not in the daytime . . . I can't, I can't!" And she fell to her knees like the heroines in the Yiddish theater. She embraced the calves of his legs, kissing his pants, the cuffs.

Max pulled her up by the hair and a shoulder. "I'll lower the shades."

"Have pity, no!" Basha wheezed.

"Well, a stubborn one, then!"

Max pushed and shoved her. She fell backward toward the bed but managed to remain on her feet. Her hair, which she had combed earlier, became wildly disheveled again. Her face looked puffy and swollen. She was seized with a coughing fit, sobbed, quivered, forced out a single word again and again that he did not understand, like the rebellious babbling of a child.

"Well, it's not meant to be," Max said to himself. He went over to the faucet and put the temporary compress on his face. It started to hurt and he murmured, "What a slob, that small-town scullion, that Wyszkower cunt . . ." Words came to his lips that he had long since forgotten. He still had the strength and the desire to conquer, but the little place in his head that had the last word said no. She would start screaming and the hotel staff would come. He hadn't returned to Warsaw to rot in prison.

He took off the compress with its traces of blood, poured water on it, wrung it out, and put it on his face. One eye remained uncovered and he looked behind him.

Basha was gazing at him with awe, supplication, and curiosity. Her lips moved but no words came out. Now for the first time he realized what he had done. He had ripped her dress from neck to bosom. A part of her undershirt was hanging out.

How will she go home? Max wondered. Is it possible to get her another dress? And what will her mistress say? It suddenly occurred to Max: Perhaps I should take her away, right now, just as she is.

"Do you want to go to America with me? I mean now!"

Basha's face lit up. "To America? On the Sabbath?"

"You can go to America even on Yom Kippur."

"You are laughing at me. Laughing!"

"I tore your clothes. How will you go home in a torn dress?"

"I'll pin it."

She went over to the chair where her purse was lying and dug out a few safety pins.

"It's forbidden to do this on the Sabbath," she murmured, "but—"

He stood and watched as she fixed her dress. "Right after the Sabbath I'll buy you another dress, or maybe I'll give you money and you'll buy it yourself or let someone sew a dress for you."

"I don't have to buy a dress. I can fix this one so no one will know."

"I'll buy you a new dress. When will we see each other again?"

"I have a day off only once every two weeks."

"What day will that be?"

"This Wednesday."

Max arranged a meeting with her. He helped her put on her hat. After that he began to kiss her again and she returned his kisses. She cried out something, but he didn't understand what. Her face became hot and his cheeks damp. He pressed her to his chest and once more felt full of lust and sure of his powers. He said, "Now you must be mine."

Basha didn't want to ride in a droshky on the Sabbath, but she had difficulty walking. Clinging to Max's arm, she took small steps and protested, "I can't go back to them. Oh, look what has happened to me!"

"If you want, I'll take a room for you in a hotel and you won't have to show your face there anymore," Max said.

"What hotel? What are you talking about? I have all my things there. They owe me for the season. Besides that, what'll I do in a hotel? I'm used to working."

"You'll work yet, don't worry. Everything will turn out fine. Remember, from now on you are in my hands. Whatever I tell you, you'll do."

"When are you going back to whatever you call it, in America?"

"Maybe in a few weeks. Maybe in a few months."

"Well, it was all fated. I dreamed about you the whole night as I lay squirming on my bed like a snake. On the Sabbath I don't have to get up early, but by six o'clock I was up. I was afraid you wouldn't like my hat and everything else. Did you cast a magic spell over me or what?"

"There was no spell."

"What will become of me? From childhood on, my grandmother used to warn me, 'Watch out for men. A man can be your best friend, but he is your enemy.' Those were her words."

"Believe me, you don't have a better friend."

"Who? My mother is dead. My father—may he be well—is a stubborn man. You can't get a word out of him. When I come home for the holidays, he asks, 'How are you?' And before I can answer he's back to the Gemara. I didn't descend out of a garbage heap. My grandfather Reb Mordkhele studied from a Gemara as big as a table."

"Was he also a teacher in a cheder?"

"He taught boys of marriageable age."

He was supposed to be at Reyzl Kork's at seven o'clock, but the clock in the town hall already showed twenty to eight. Basha's steps became slower and slower. Her face was pale. She leaned on his shoulder shivering, halting every few steps.

Again and again Max proposed taking a droshky, but each time she repeated that she didn't want to ride on the Sabbath. "I have committed enough sins already without that," she said.

They fell silent and didn't talk the rest of the way until Gnoyna Street. Max's head was full of thoughts. Could it be that Shkolnikov helped him? Could it be that the telepathic messages that he had sent Rochelle had removed the curse? He had suffered for two years, spent a fortune on doctors, medicines, and baths, but nothing helped. Suddenly a redheaded servant girl appeared and redeemed him. Was he happy now?

There were times when he thought that if only he were free of his trouble, he would be the most fortunate of men. Yet here he was crawling through the Warsaw streets, inwardly quiet, lonely, and pensive. He looked at the shops that were closed for the Sabbath, the parading couples, the Jews in satin coats, velvet hats, and fur-trimmed hats who were undoubtedly going to the Hasidic studyhouses for their prayers, followed by young boys with curly sidelocks in *saklekh*—six-cornered hats. The shining sun was already red with a hint of night. On the doorsteps old women wearing long earrings were sitting in caps and old-fashioned garments.

Somehow it was as if Max were trying to listen to himself. He had spoken of love to both Tsirele and Basha, but was he really in love? Can you love two women at the same time? Tsirele seemed far away to him now; Basha's silence and slow pace irritated him. She was beginning to hang on to him like a wife. She was already putting on airs. He looked sideways at her. "She's just as miserable and mixed up as I am." She kept her eyes down, teetering on her high heels, and he just about had to drag her.

Max realized full well that he had very little reason to worry about arriving late at Reyzl Kork's. Of what consequence was lateness in comparison with what had just happened to him? Furthermore, what did he need Reyzl Kork for? He had come to Warsaw seeking a cure for his nerves, not to become a flesh peddler. But his nature was such that he couldn't stand keeping someone waiting. She had surely prepared supper and was now sitting there, expecting him.

At the end of Gnoyna Street Basha said to him, "Now I have to go home by myself. All I need is for them to see me with you."

"All right, go if you like. We'll meet Wednesday opposite the armory and you can bring your things and never go back to them anymore."

"Where will you take me Wednesday? No, I'll continue serving until we go to America."

"Let it be so."

"Where are you going now?"

Max almost said, To Reyzl Kork's, but he realized that this would not be wise. A girl like Basha could already be jealous.

"Back to the hotel."

"You're not going to eat the last meal of the Sabbath?"

"I'll eat something."

"The old woman will probably give me what for. If I'm a minute late she's ready to eat me alive."

"Let her go to hell. From now on you'll be more of a lady than she is."

Basha frowned; her mouth twisted into a grimace. "Do you think she'll know?"

"Nobody can tell anything."

"Well, a good Sabbath. I didn't know it would turn out like this . . . as God is my witness."

Max kissed her on the cheek. She gave him a look full of accusation and turned into Krochmalna Street. Max went out of his way but walked quickly and paced it so that he would arrive at No. 23 before Basha. He practically ran. He hurried past Gnoyna Street, came out on Grzybowska, and turned into Ciepla. He must get to No. 23 before Basha. An encounter with her in the courtyard would spoil everything. When he got to Krochmalna Street, he began to look in the direction from which Basha should be coming, but he didn't see her.

It was already getting dark. His watch showed that it was close to nine. He went up the stairs that led to Reyzl Kork's place and caught his breath. He stopped and wiped the sweat off his face. The thought occurred to him that his whole life had been devoted to cheating and stealing. As a boy he had stolen from his parents and sometimes from strangers. Later he had become a thief by trade. Then he began to steal love, or whatever else you want to name it. He always had to go by way of back alleys, find pretexts, think up excuses, deceive women. He could rarely pass a street without being afraid that he might bump into someone he wouldn't want to meet, or be seen with someone he shouldn't be seen with.

Outwitting such a wily one as Rochelle was not so simple. She knew him through and through and was aware of his devious ways. As long as she was young enough and pretty enough, he had no need to be involved with others. Nevertheless he couldn't get along without intrigues and lies. Remnants of old love affairs survived from which he found it hard to disengage himself. Rochelle was his business partner, but he always made deals that she knew nothing about; he had hidden bank accounts she was not aware of. And now, after having been in Warsaw only a week, he had got himself so deeply embroiled that he would never get out. "Well, that's what I am, that's Max Barabander for you!"

He knocked at the door and Reyzl opened it, saying, "I began to think you weren't coming. Come on in."

She led him into the center of the room, where a table was set for two. Evidently Reyzl cooked on the Sabbath, for Max detected the odors of cutlets, a schav-borscht, and new potatoes. The lamps weren't lit yet, but the setting sun threw purple shadows on the wall. Reyzl looked at him for a while with her black eyes. Then she said, "So you seduced her."

"What makes you think that?"

"She scratched your forehead and you came two hours late."

Max didn't answer and Reyzl looked thoughtful. After a while she said, "By force it's no good."

"I didn't rape her."

"Sit down. I didn't turn on the gas lamps because if that busybody who lives across the street should see me light them on the Sabbath, she'd come across the street to punish me. We'll soon be able to turn on the lights."

"For my part it can remain dark."

"Are you hungry? Where is Basha?"

"She went home."

"You didn't have to rush," said Reyzl amicably. "She wouldn't have disappeared."

He didn't answer and she went into the kitchen. He sat down on the sofa and felt his tiredness. He stretched out, sure that Reyzl would come right back. But time passed and she didn't return. The purple shadows vanished and the room became dark. Max closed his eyes and fell asleep.

He dreamed that he was in prison. Was it in Buenos Aires

or in Warsaw? Other prisoners were sitting there and he hoped to learn from their responses, in Polish or Spanish, where he was. They all remained mute in an eerie silence. Suddenly an old woman appeared and she held a rope with a noose. Is she a hangman? Max wondered. How can a woman be a hangman? The old woman winked at him and fanned herself with the rope. The prisoners stared at him stony-faced. This is the end, thought Max. He began to say the prayer "Hear, O Israel," and woke up.

The lamps were burning. Reyzl brought in two plates of schav-borscht, saying, "She exhausted you, then?"

"What kind of dream was that?" Max asked himself. He barely heard Reyzl's words and didn't fully grasp their meaning. Reyzl showed him to the chair at the head of the table, the place where Shmuel Smetena had last sat. Max got up and felt his knees buckling under him. Am I so old and worn out? he wondered. He sat down in Shmuel's place and began slurping the borscht. He hadn't eaten since one o'clock and suddenly realized how hungry he was. He ate the new potatoes garnished with melted butter and chopped parsley greens, and with every bite his strength returned. Reyzl chewed and looked at him piercingly with her black eyes.

"I wanted you to come to me fresh," she said, "not all used up."

"The Americans say, 'Business before pleasure,' " Max replied.

"Oh? I didn't know you were such a keen businessman."

"Well, don't you want your percentage?"

Reyzl seemed taken aback and Max knew that he was stronger than she was, sure of himself. She knew it, too, and was a bit afraid of him. Once more he had the upper hand over the female sex.

"You're as likely to make money from this rotten business as a pig is to see its own tail," he said to himself. "All you'll do is cuckold Shmuel Smetena."

Max finished his potato, took a last spoonful of borscht, and Reyzl cleared the table.

"Where's your maid?" Max asked.

"I sent her away to visit her mother in Pelcowizna. She won't be back until Monday morning."

"You're well prepared."

"Everything has to be planned." Reyzl had already gone to the door of the corridor leading into the kitchen when she turned around and said, "You shouldn't have started up with the rabbi's daughter."

Max didn't answer right away. "It's not your business."

"Since you have a wife in Buenos Aires, you have no business playing the role of suitor."

Reyzl went into the kitchen, her heels clicking on the wooden floorboards. In that one moment it became clear to Max that Reyzl was riding the horse, not he. She could even squeal on him to the cops. She could set those thugs in the square on him. Then again, if Shmuel Smetena found out that she had cheated on him, he might kill her.

"Well, it's a game like all games," Max comforted himself. He wasn't afraid, but he realized he was risking his life. What if Shmuel Smetena found out that he had slept here overnight? The dream about the prisoners, the old woman, and the rope came to mind and he thought, I must take my revolver wherever I go.

In a few hours everything was over—the delicious supper, the kissing and caressing before going to bed, the discussions of how Max was going to deliver Basha to Reyzl's sister, Señora Shayevsky. While it was satisfying for Max to feel the return of his former virility after two years of impotence, it had ended up with his turning his face to the wall. After that, Reyzl said a few more words and gave a little snort. "A person can feel hunger for years," Max said to himself, "but as soon as you eat one satisfying meal you are satiated." He fell asleep and woke up an hour and a half later. It took awhile before he remembered where he was. He had touched a woman and asked himself, "Where am I? Is this Rochelle? No, it's not Rochelle. Am I in London? Berlin?" In a moment he remembered everything: he was in Warsaw in Shmuel Smetena's apartment and, thank God, his sickness was a thing of the past.

Again he felt as if he were looking into his own inner depths, and again he found no clear answer.

"Crazy, crazy," Max muttered. This Reyzl Kork was certainly a ball of fire, but he had no intention of taking such a character home with him. The more he thought about it, the more he realized that the only reason he had gotten involved in all these escapades was because of his impotence. He couldn't divorce Rochelle, nor would he leave his business to become a world traveler. Besides, he had gone through half the money he had with him and there was only one way out—to return to Argentina. Now that he had been released from the magic spell that had been cast upon him, he would find plenty of women in Argentina. He had wronged Tsirele and Basha, but it would be better for both of them if he were to take himself off before he also dragged them down into the muck. Tomorrow morning

I'll leave Warsaw, Max decided. He had only one worry. Reyzl Kork would probably inform her sister of everything, and she would malign him in Argentina. But why should he be afraid of her, and after all, what could she do to him?

Max's anxiety had kept him in a constant state of intoxication. Now he was sober. He had turned his face to the wall, and opening his eyes a slit, he could see that it was beginning to brighten toward dawn. From time to time a bird would chirp and then fall silent. Max dozed off again. Before he fell asleep he asked himself, "Should I go to Roszkow?" And his reply was "No." The rabbi and Tsirele knew about Roszkow and they could track him down there. The best thing was to take the express train to Berlin and then to Paris. He had a passport and visas and they wouldn't send any couriers after him.

Max slept for an hour or two or maybe three. When he awoke, the sun was shining through the partially lowered window shades. He saw Reyzl lying at the edge of the bed, sleeping peacefully, quietly, scarcely breathing. Max studied her face. Already not so young, but not as faded as Rochelle, who smeared her face with all kinds of creams. Reyzl's face was free of lotions.

Max thought of Argentina, where it was winter now, rainy and cold, where the stoves, used only for cooking, left even the richest families shivering. The return from Warsaw to London and then the month-long journey to Argentina seemed unbearable to Max. "Why not take that Basha along?" Max asked himself. "Why return to that earlier emptiness?" His nerves were tormenting him. One moment they were quiet, the next they were agitated as if by an internal demon who gets inside a person and plays tricks on him. Just when you think you've vanquished the demons, they stick out their tongues.

Max made a new resolution: he would go away with Basha.

Of course it wouldn't be easy. Even if Basha agreed to leave her masters, Reyzl Kork would find out and could put obstacles in his path. A woman like that could squeal on him to the police, or hire thugs and blackmailers. Well, how could he get in touch with Basha now? Basha had given him her telephone number but had warned him that if the old man or old woman answered they wouldn't call her to the telephone. They might even take away her day off. After giving it some thought, Max decided to wait until Wednesday, when Basha had agreed to meet him. How long would it be until Wednesday? He would speak to her plainly: Either come along or remain sweating here in Warsaw. By Wednesday the girl would be missing him. He would take her to the border at Mlawa. Twenty years earlier he and a smuggler had stolen across the border to Germany. He knew the route. Once there, everything would go smoothly. He would rent an apartment for Basha and she would become his mistress, Spanish style. He would have two homes, one with Basha and one with Rochelle. The girl wasn't accustomed to luxury and she wouldn't cost him too much. A girl like her would also be faithful. Maybe at one point he could have a child with her, it occurred to Max. Even though Rochelle no longer had that choice, he could still produce an heir, someone he could leave his fortune to.

After Max came to this decision, he wondered how he could have decided earlier to run away alone. It would have been madness. Why leave behind a young woman and start roaming alone again over the high seas? Why return to a cold winter and old troubles? Max had to re-explain all this to himself: "It's not good to be drunk, but it's also not good to be too sober."

What should he do until his Wednesday meeting with Basha? He had promised to see Tsirele again on Monday after the midday dinner. The rabbi and the rebbetzin considered him engaged. I'll have to play that role one more time, Max thought. One thing I can forget about now is going to that sorcerer Shkolnikov.

Max lay there for a long time, neither asleep nor quite awake. Then he remembered that the rabbi could place a curse on him for shaming his daughter. Jews like him have a say in the heavens. If such a man cursed him, he would remain accursed in this world and the next. Aside from that, it's a terrible thing to hurt such a saintly man. Maybe I could leave him money, a hundred or several hundred rubles? Max thought. Well, and what about Tsirele? She's a delicate child, and not too stable. She's already tried to jump off the balcony; she could fall into a depression and he, Max, would be the cause of her death. Even Reyzl Kork had warned him against getting involved with the rabbi's daughter. Money? A woman like Tsirele can't be bought off with money.

Max was tired, but no matter how many times he closed his eyes, they opened again. He imagined what would happen when Tsirele and her parents learned of his flight. Tsirele would cry, faint, try to throw herself out the window. Her father and mother would hold her back. Reyzl would inform the rabbi that he had a wife in Argentina. The rabbi would curse him with deadly curses. What did they call it in Roszkow? The Chapter of Curses. Reyzl Kork would send a letter to her sister that Max had posed as a single man and was engaged to the rabbi's daughter. Rochelle would learn what he'd done. They would talk about him in the cafés. He would be thrown out of the Burial Society. He wouldn't be allowed into a synagogue on Rosh Hashanah and Yom Kippur. It would hurt his business, too. Nobody would want to buy houses and lots from "an unclean one." He closed his eyes and fell asleep. Reyzl woke him up. She had changed into a petticoat and slippers. Shaking him by the shoulders, she said, "Sleepyhead, it's nine o'clock."

Max looked at her with scorn. She had sworn that she was faithful to Shmuel Smetena, but not when Max came around. He was lying in her bed, with Reyzl waking him and tickling him under the arm, her black eyes smiling at him knowingly, with deceitfulness and without a trace of shame or regret. There's always a ready customer for someone else's wife.

"Go out and I'll get dressed."

"You're ashamed, eh? I'll get breakfast ready."

Max got out of bed. He was wearing Shmuel Smetena's nightshirt, much too big for him. The bathroom was in the corridor, where Max stood touching the growth of stubble on his face. Recently his beard had grown with extraordinary rapidity. Though he shaved in the morning, by evening his chin was prickly, and the next morning his chin felt like a grater. Reyzl saw him and started laughing.

"Why are you laughing, eh?"

"Two of you can fit into that nightshirt. He really let himself go. Come in and wash up. I promise I won't look."

"I'll just wash my hands and face."

"We don't have a bath. This isn't the Hotel Bristol."

Max washed up and got a whiff of coffee and freshly boiled milk. Whenever he visited a woman, he would take a toothbrush, a nightshirt, and a bathrobe with him, but recently he had lost his male confidence. He now washed his face and rinsed his mouth with water at the sink. He touched the stubble on his beard and experienced the same qualms he had felt in his youth when he had been with a prostitute. From his boyhood he felt anger toward these women who sold themselves. The more they perfumed themselves, the more they stank. When he paid them, he felt a desire to spit in their faces. Nevertheless, he had married one of that kind. Along with lust for her, he had felt regret and disgust over Rochelle's sordid past. At the same time he had a craving to hear all the stories he dragged out of her. However, after Arturo's death, when Rochelle locked herself up in an impenetrable fortress, every time he tried to get close to her, she would say, "Leave me alone. I am old and broken. Go to whomever you want." Nevertheless, she wouldn't divorce him. She had become money-hungry and cunning. It was a miracle that he had been able to put away some money without her knowledge.

Max had barely managed to get dressed when Reyzl came in and asked, "What's the matter? Is something hurting you, or what?"

"Nothing hurts me."

"Since you've gotten up, you seem different. Is it my fault?"

"No, Reyzl, it's not your fault."

"If you're yearning for Basha, I can get her for you."

"I'm not yearning for anyone."

"Come and eat. God knows, I didn't want to do it. If you hadn't turned up, I would have muddled through the years with him."

"What do you want to do now? Leave him?"

Reyzl looked at Max coolly. "I'm not the jealous type, but break it off with Tsirele. Everyone knows about it."

"Who's talking about it?"

"Everybody. You even went to pray with the rabbi. You shouldn't do that, Max. You'll destroy the whole family. For that you have to have the heart of a murderer."

·　·　·

During the years when Max was running from one doctor to another, they assured him that he wasn't suffering from any organic illness. Yet all around him people who had looked strong and healthy were suddenly discovered to have diseased kidneys and livers. Many died of diabetes or bad hearts, gallstones or cancer. Not a week passed without his going to a funeral with Rochelle. Doctors wrote that people in Argentina were eating too much meat and too much sugar. Almost all his old acquaintances, friends, and lovers had died, many of whom were his own age. What's the use of money when the Angel of Death is ready to strike you down? What's the point of life's pleasures when in the blink of an eye you can be carried away to the cemetery? It's no wonder that rascals called the Burial Society the most "alive" of all the community organizations in Buenos Aires. There was a time when all this ruminating had thrown Max into a deep depression. In the past two years other thoughts had tortured him, but the fear of death lurked constantly. He woke up in the morning with a coated tongue. At times he had pains in his chest, cramps in his stomach, his ears didn't hear as clearly as they used to, and when he climbed a few stairs, he felt breathless.

After Max had taken leave of Reyzl Kork, he made a new resolve to take care of his health. What would happen if he was to fall sick in this foreign country? He would be hospitalized among Gentiles and wouldn't even be able to make himself understood to the doctor or the nurse. If he died, no one would know where his bones were buried. "Today I won't go to Tsirele or to Shkolnikov. I'll go straight to the hotel."

When he went through the gate, he turned in the direction of Ciepla Street, but his feet, moving as if directed by some outer force, turned the other way. He passed No. 10 and glanced up at the rabbi's balcony. He looked to see whether Esther, the baker woman, might be standing at the gate at No. 15. When he passed Haym Kaviornik's café, he made a motion as if to enter but instead went into the tavern at No. 6. Maybe Blind Mayer, whose name he had heard over twenty years ago, would be sitting there. In truth, Max had a yen to talk to a man.

In the front room, where the bar stood, it was noisy. Youths in britches and high boots, with hats pulled down over their eyes, girls with pockmarked and ravaged faces crowded together in one bunch. Max pushed through the crowd and went into the other room, which was half empty. He saw a big, broad-shouldered fellow with a huge head, a crooked scar on his low forehead, one empty eye socket, and a red bulbous nose. He was powerfully built and his face was pitted with scars. So this was Blind Mayer, King of Krochmalna Street, rabbi of the underworld! Max gave a little cough and Blind Mayer straightened up slowly, like an ox. From under his thick eyebrows he looked at Max suspiciously with his one good eye. His glance was full of the bitterness of those who no longer expect anything good to happen to them.

"Is that you, Mayer?" said Max.

"Who are you?" Blind Mayer asked in a rasping voice that rumbled up from his bowels.

"You won't know. My name is Max Barabander and I come from Buenos Aires. An old friend of yours, Hatskele Peltes, sends you his greetings through me."

Blind Mayer thought for a long time. His lips, lined by two deep furrows, were trembling.

"I know, I know. He's in Buenos Aires, but people said he died."

"He'll never die."

"What's he doing?"

"He's become a rich man."

Blind Mayer laid his fist on the table. "How long is it since he left Warsaw? It must be ten years."

"More like twenty."

"Is that right? Time passes quickly. I remember him. He used to go around with a blond girl."

"Hanetche. Now she's his wife."

"So he married her? I'm surprised that he still remembers me. The world has passed Blind Mayer by, forgotten him like he was dead."

"He talks about you often."

"What does he say? Sit down, don't stand. If you're hungry go over to the bar and get something to eat. Once there was a waiter here, but they fired him. You have to get everything yourself from the girl. The food in this saloon is junk!" said Blind Mayer, grimacing with anger and disgust.

"I'm not hungry," Max said. "If *you* want something, then we can go into the tavern at No. 17."

"To Lazar? Yes, I want to, but the doctor has ordered me not to. I'm not even allowed to drink a glass of beer. I have ulcers!" said Blind Mayer, pointing to his belly, which stuck out over the table.

"Maybe you want to go over to Haym Kaviornik's. He has good cheese buns."

"Cheese buns, eh? Biscuits with milk. That I can eat," said Mayer, pushing down his lower lip so that a few long black crooked hooklike teeth appeared. He sat awhile shaking his head as if he were at a funeral. Then he asked, "What does Peltes do there?"

"He has a knitwear factory."

"A factory, Hatskele Peltes the rat?"

"A big factory with over fifty workers. Mostly Spanish women."

"Well, and she?"

"Quite the lady."

"Psh! They go away to America and become respectable. She was a whore right here in No. 6. Itchele Glomp was her pimp."

"She looks like a countess. You should see her diamonds!" Max showed with his thumb that they measured half his index finger.

Blind Mayer banged his other fist on the table. "What do they know in America? Everything there is money. If you've got the cash, you can ride the horse. Here there was rioting and the old gang was knocked off. I sit here and don't know anybody. People talk to me and I don't know who they are. During the riots the shoemakers and tailors ganged up on us. There was nobody to fight back. Everybody on the square was beaten up. They scattered like rabbits. The workers went into the whorehouses and beat up the girls. Twenty bastards attacked me, and with twenty against one, no one's a big shot. They took me away to the hospital in Czyste and I lay there six weeks. Nobody outside of two or three people even came to see how I was doing. That's Krochmalna Street today. And on Smocza Street it's no better. Why are you here?"

"No reason. Came to look at old-time Warsaw."

"It's not the old Warsaw anymore. Gone, buried. Once everyone had his own territory. Now the worst lowlife comes here. Nobody knows anybody else. This one says black, the other says white. Then there's a raid. They catch them and put them in the paddy wagon like dogs. In my day, Commissar

Voynov drank brandy with us. The sergeant used to bow to me and show me respect, may I live to be buried in a Jewish cemetery. There was a Leybush Trelbukh here, and if he made a promise, it was as if it had been written down in a book. He would go to the police station and say, 'Your Excellency, this is one of my people,' and the man would immediately be released from the jailhouse. It's thirty-six years since Leybush died. What am I saying? More like forty. He used to come to me and say, 'Mayer, thus and such happened. They locked up a father of children and he must be pulled out.' In ten minutes there was a pile of money. We got to the chief of police or my name is not Mayer."

"Yes, I know."

"What do you know? Nothing. What's the name of the city where you live?"

"Buenos Aires."

"I know. They used to send shiploads there. There's still one of the old guard around here, Shmuel Smetena. At one time he was a fence, now he's a big shot. He lives with a woman who has a sister in Buenos Aires."

"I know who you mean. She's not such a big fish there."

"What do I know? What's her sister called? Reyzl Kork. Up until the riots, she was standing at the gate here on Krochmalna Street calling out to the drunks. But Shmuel Smetena fell head over heels in love with her and left his wife. He rented an apartment for her at No. 23 and she's the boss. What does today's generation know? But Blind Mayer has a mind and he remembers. With me they are all marked down. They can't fool me. That's why they hate me."

"Nobody hates you. On the contrary."

"Well, well. They hate me. I'm telling you the truth, and for the truth you get a beating. But why should I be afraid of them? What can they do to me? Chase my ducks off the water? I sit here the whole day and life goes by me like a dream. Every few minutes there's a brawl. A Gentile goes by and they snatch his wallet. The whores have to go for inspection every month. Everything is written on the yellow pass. If a woman gets the little black worm, they ship her off to the hospital, where they poison her and don't even give her a funeral. They dig a hole and put Jews in there together with Gentiles. Once a pimp disguised himself as a woman. When the paddy wagon comes, they all run off. All they want is a few groschen, the Devil take their hides. So how is it in Buenos Aires?"

"The Spaniard will sell his own wife so that he can walk around doing nothing."

"I hear that there are black people there."

"In America, not in Argentina."

"In New York, then?"

"In New York, in Chicago, in Cleveland."

"Were you there?"

"Several times."

"How is life there? They wanted me to go, but who went to America in those days? Only the dregs. I lacked nothing here. On Krochmalna Street, on Smocza Street, in the whole district I was boss. They came to me from Tamke, from Szilits, from Powazki, from Ochota. My word was the law. All the discontent came from the strikers. Alexander was a good Tsar but they killed him. Then the pogroms started and people began running away to far-off lands. They began to ask for a Duma, but what's the good of a Duma when you have no money and your life is a misery? The Duma did them as much good as it does to cup a corpse. A shoemaker stayed a shoemaker and a general a general. Am I right or not?"

"You're right."

"It's no good when you get old. I sit here the whole day because it's hard for me to walk. From lying down, you get sores. No matter what you do, it's not worth a damn. Do you have a wife?"

"Yes, I do."

"Why did you come here? Looking for a sweetheart?"

"You can get one there, too."

"And how! There's no lack of that kind of goods anywhere. But when you get old and your bones ache, it doesn't even come to mind. You could put the Queen of Sheba in front of me naked and I wouldn't even look at her. I've had more women than you can imagine. Once I went to a city and I stayed at a hotel. Next to me, right next door, was a colonel and his wife. I got to talking to her and she fell head over heels in love with me—just like that, suddenly. She came into my room and began to talk. I told her the truth: 'I have a thousand to choose from.' She became white as chalk and said, 'They don't love you, but I love you.' 'How do I know that you're telling me the truth?' I was smoking a cigarette and she says, 'Give me your cigarette.' I give her the cigarette and she presses the burning end into her hand and burns a hole in her flesh. It even turned black. 'Here's your sign,' she says. In all my life I never saw such a thing. I wanted to run to the apothecary to get some salve, but she said, '*Nichevo*. Give me your mouth,' and she sucked me like a leech. For three days and nights I stayed in the hotel with this Russian woman. We ate and slept, nothing else. When I got out the fourth day, I could barely walk. I felt like someone who has had typhoid fever."

"What did she do? Go back to the colonel?"

"To who else, then? To you? There were maneuvers in the area and he took her with him. Have you ever heard of anything like this?"

"Never."

"The longer you live, the more you learn. You think you know it all, but suddenly you hear something and you can't believe your ears. It's even mentioned somewhere in a holy book, I don't remember where."

The morning had passed. A hotel clerk came to notify Max that someone was calling him on the telephone, but he told him to say he was not in. He lay for hours on the bed dozing, tired by his conquests. Tsirele was looking for him, but he decided to wait it out until Wednesday. He no longer wanted or felt able to talk to Tsirele. He was afraid of her intelligent talk, of her mother's angry glances, and above all of the rabbi. Max knew for sure that if the rabbi cursed him, the curse would come to pass. Max could no longer continue to deceive Tsirele with talk of marrying her, when he already had a wife. With Basha it was another story; her father lived in the provinces with his wife and children and Max was safe.

At nine o'clock in the evening he came out of his dream state, awakened by hunger. The sun, which hadn't set yet, stood there red and huge, almost touching the earth, separated by only a thin strip of clouds. For the first time since he had come to Warsaw, Max prepared to spend a night alone. He walked the length of New World Street, found a coffeehouse, and ordered rolls, herring, an omelet, and coffee. He tried to read a Polish newspaper, but he couldn't read that language anymore. He picked up an illustrated journal from another table and looked at the pictures. He had no need to read the captions: a well-known general and yet another general; here a beautiful actress and there a princess; a bride holding a bouquet at a wedding and a groom leaning on the handle of his sword. They all wanted the same things—money, a mate, power. But alas, what were his accomplishments? People like him had to live with remnants, pick up what others threw away, what no one wanted. Even Tsirele was too much for him. He had come out of rubbish and there he must remain.

He ate slowly so that the time spent on his meal wouldn't pass too quickly. He sipped his coffee from a spoon. He read an article in which he understood only one line out of three. Now he was sorry he had slept the day away, because he wouldn't be able to sleep till dawn. He smoked one cigarette after another. I made a mistake, he thought. I should have gone to the séance. He put his hand in his inside coat pocket and took out his address book, which he had carried with him since he came to Warsaw. He began to leaf through it, reading names that were entirely strange to him while others were familiar. Probably none of the people for whom he brought greetings from Argentina had a telephone. Nevertheless, the address book cheered him up a bit.

He sat in the café until eleven o'clock, then walked back to the hotel. At the end of Chmielna Street, prostitutes tried to entice him. For a moment Max thought that he would stop and have a chat with them, but they spoke Polish, not Yiddish. He returned to the hotel, but instead of going to his room, he sat in the lobby. An old woman with a yellow face in a black hat trailing a black veil was scolding a young girl of about seventeen. The old woman's blue lips were quivering. She seemed angry and was giving the girl a piece of her mind. White hairs sprouted from her chin. The girl listened without even trying to answer. Max didn't take his eyes off them. What difference did it make to this old woman how this girl behaved? How long could this dried-up body wander about on this earth? Nobody, it seems, thinks about death. Not even such a broken shard as this. What would happen if he knew for sure that in six months he would be dead? What could he actually do?

Max became totally absorbed in this train of thought. What would he do if he had only one year to live? You can't lie down in bed and wait for the end. You have to do something. Would he divide his fortune among the poor? First he would have to go back to Argentina and sell his houses and lots. It would be a year before everything he owned could be converted to cash. And on what basis could you conclude that charity helps? There's no other world; a dead man is like a dead ox.

There was only one pleasure for a man like him: women. He would try to have as many women as possible. He wouldn't spare any money. He would take on as many as he could. Suppose he had only one year to live.

Was tonight lost? Should he telephone Reyzl Kork and tell her that he wanted to stay over? Should he try to see Esther, the baker woman, again? He felt that he didn't have the energy for sexual adventures. Even if you have only a year to live, you can't do more than your strength will bear. Should he go to a bar and get drunk? No, he didn't have a desire for whiskey. Smoke another cigarette? Tonight was lost. But what should he do tomorrow?

Sitting in the armchair, Max began to work out a plan. He

would bring over as much money as he could from Argentina. He would keep switching women. With one year to live, you wouldn't have to worry about someone's curses. He would travel all over the world and bring a slew of women with him. With lots of money you can get everything. Well, he would have to have someone to assist him—a secretary, a broker, an intimate who would help him carry out the whole plan. But who?

In a flash he knew—Reyzl Kork! She was tired of Shmuel Smetena and she loved money. She would procure not one Basha for him but fifty. He would travel around the world with them and pay Reyzl a salary. She would go back to Argentina with him. She would want to see her sister.

Max was used to fantasizing, but he had never been as taken with a fantasy as by this one. He wouldn't have to spend his entire fortune. Fifteen or twenty thousand rubles would cover all his expenses. He didn't need any showgirls. Girls like Basha would be good enough for him. If God were to grant him more years, he would hardly be left a pauper.

Yes, that's what I'll do, Max decided. He had an urge to call Reyzl Kork and talk to her. He got up to look for a telephone but then immediately sat down again. No, not now. He would think everything through, work out a plan as an architect does before he builds a house, or an engineer who first draws a blueprint for a machine. He would do everything in such a way that Rochelle couldn't start a lawsuit against him.

Max took a look around. The old woman and the girl, her granddaughter or great-granddaughter, had left. He remained alone in the lobby. He went over to the clerk and took his key. He didn't take the elevator and slowly climbed up the red-carpeted marble stairs. Without turning on the light, he lay down in his clothes on the bed. Yes, he had earned a year's happiness after the years of sorrow and sickness brought on by Arturo's death.

He knew that Reyzl Kork would seize on his plans. During the night he had spent with her, Max had come to understand her situation. Shmuel Smetena was old and fat; he loved beer, not women. He had little patience for love. Around two o'clock, when Max fell asleep, he had just about thought everything through. He would travel with Reyzl and she would procure girls for him everywhere. She was a born madam. Actually Reyzl had proposed this plan at their first meeting. Women like her were not jealous; in fact, procuring women became a passion with them.

Max fell asleep. When he opened his eyes, the sun was shining and his clock showed ten to seven. He had slept only five hours but he awoke feeling refreshed. Max arose sure that he had found a way out of all his entanglements. He needed a partner for his adventures, someone who would help him and would enjoy being with him—Reyzl Kork. She had found Basha for him, and that was just the beginning.

It was too early to call Reyzl, so Max shaved at the sink. He called the maid and ordered a bath. Then he got dressed and went down to breakfast. "The two of us can turn the world upside down," Max said to himself. "She herself isn't a bad piece of goods either." Was it possible that Reyzl would say no? "Impossible," Max answered himself. "Unless the rabbi interferes." He must make it up to him and give him a dowry for Tsirele.

At nine o'clock Max rang Reyzl Kork. When he heard her voice, she sounded overjoyed.

"Max, I thought about you half the night."

"Which half, the first or the second?"

"In between."

"Reyzl, I have to talk to you."

"Well, talk. You have a mouth, thank goodness."

"Maybe we can meet."

"Why not? I've nothing to do. I miss you."

"That's all I want to know. When shall I come?"

"Now."

"That's how a woman should talk. I'm coming right away."

"Have you had breakfast yet?"

"Yes."

"Well, we'll eat a second breakfast."

"That's it. That's what I was looking for," Max said aloud to himself. "She'll do everything I want. For one year I must feel a zest for life!"

He locked his door and went out. He felt so light that he skipped down the steps. When he got outside, he saw Tsirele. He was so taken aback that he looked at her, unable to speak. Tsirele was wearing the hat he had bought her and a gray suit. She was pale. Max was stricken with fear.

"Tsirele, what are you doing here?" he asked.

She looked at him with a measured glance and a sort of angry smile.

"Where are you going so early in the morning?" she asked. "I didn't sleep a wink. I didn't even shut my eyes. Max, I have to talk to you."

"Well, come."

"I can't talk in the street."

"Come up to my room."

"No, Max, I'm not going up to a man's room."

"Then we'll stay downstairs in the lobby."

"Perhaps we can go somewhere where it's quiet?"

"Where is it quiet? In the grave," said Max, surprised at his own words.

"Let's go to the Saxony Gardens. In the morning it's quiet there."

"Agreed."

He held her under the arm and she did not pull away. They walked slowly and silently like a married couple. They came to the gardens, to the section called the Eleven Gates, and walked in. Max realized that he now owed Tsirele a clear explanation, but he didn't know what he would say. He bowed his head. His whole life was a game played against a hidden enemy, a real devil. It wasn't Tsirele but the other one, the Evil One, who paradoxically thwarted him in his pursuit of those pleasures he had been chasing since he was old enough to stand on his feet.

ell, you can't make a fur hat
out of a pig's tail," Max said to himself. He should never have
dared think about marrying Tsirele. It was madness, madness.
He had finally told her the truth, that he had a wife in Buenos
Aires. She had spit at him, and he did not even wipe off the
spittle with a handkerchief. He would never forget it. Tears as
large as peas and as clear as diamonds had fallen from her eyes.
She had spoken to him in language that came from the Torah:

"Cursed may you be! Cursed forever! You shall have no
peace in this world or in the grave."

She walked and cried. At every few steps she stopped and
looked at him, her face red, tear-stained, swollen, altered. Later
Reyzl Kork had comforted him, assuring him that curses do not
come true. If a thousandth part of the curses that were leveled
at her had come to pass, she said, she would be lying dead with
her feet toward the door. But Max knew that this time the curses
would be fulfilled. It had been not only Tsirele talking but her

father the rabbi. It was his style and his voice. The words had fallen on him like red-hot stones. He actually felt them strike and burn. But he could not let remorse guide him as he waited for the bitter end. As long as he lived, he must seize a little joy. As sure as he foresaw the day of reckoning coming, that's how certain he was that he could no longer do without Reyzl Kork. In twenty-four hours she had become everything to him—wife, lover, partner, guide.

How did this all come about so quickly? Now that he had become partners with Reyzl Kork, he realized that she had pleased him all along. She was a woman with his own fantasies and wildness. She was also vivacious, experienced, and practical. They worked out a plan: Reyzl would leave Shmuel Smetena, who was old and fat, and had a wife, children, and grandchildren. He was suffering from an enlarged heart, felt sharp pains, and had attacks. What could Reyzl expect from him? He would die and not leave her a groschen.

Reyzl's sister in Argentina had written, pleading with her to emigrate. Amid the passionate kisses and wild talk that arose from lust, Reyzl threw in the fact that she was not, thank God, without a groschen: she had beautiful jewelry and had put away a little nest egg. What was the use of Max wandering around the world? If his wife, Rochelle, wouldn't divorce him, Reyzl would still live with him. If they brought a few girls like Basha with them to Argentina, they would not, God forbid, lose any money in the venture. Max could rely upon her completely.

The sky had begun to redden toward dawn, while Reyzl was still talking. Then turned away from each other and fell into a deep sleep. When Max opened his eyes, the room was full of sunlight. He awoke with a feeling of satiety and of hunger.

Reyzl was bustling about in the kitchen. Max sat up. Was this love? Yes, it was love. For the second time in his life, Max had fallen in love with a whore.

She asked him about his money and he told her everything; how much money he had, how much all his houses and lots were worth. For the first time in his life he told a woman the whole truth without hiding anything. Just as he had fooled everyone until now, so he now spent the whole night talking to Reyzl without one lie passing his mouth. He was sure that she was not fooling him. He tested her by asking if she had deceived Shmuel Smetena. Yes, in the first two years. With how many men? Reyzl remained silent. Max saw in the semidarkness that she was counting on her fingers, murmuring, "Yosele Bants, one; Chaim Kishke, two; Lame Berl, three."

"Who was the fourth, ha?"

"Wait! Leyzer Bok."

"How many altogether?"

"Eight."

"And Shmuel didn't know?"

"Not a thing!"

"And after that?"

"After that I was faithful to him for ten years, until you came. If I'm not telling the truth, may I not live out this year!" and she ran over to Max and began to cry and kiss him.

"I had pious parents," she professed. "My grandfather Reb Mendl was a trustee of a shul."

Max again laid his head on the pillow. Yes, the fathers, the grandfathers, the uncles and the aunts. They knew nothing of sin in Roszkow. When the water carrier Moishe's daughter was made pregnant by an assistant teacher, the whole town went wild. Butchers dragged the teacher out of bed, put on his pants and jacket, and locked him in a room until the wedding day. The young couple had to go away to America. Max himself had an aunt who became widowed at the age of twenty-six. She never married again and raised her five children by washing clothes. After her husband's death she never wore her wig again but only a kerchief, even on the Sabbath and holidays.

"How could it be?" Max asked himself. "Didn't blood course through their veins? Were they angels, not people? Was the fear of God so strong?"

Reyzl appeared at the door. She had never looked as lovely as she did this morning. She seemed younger, her dark eyes shining with hope and love.

"A good rising to you!" she said.

Max was taken aback. His mother—may she rest in peace—had used the very expression. "I must not leave here without visiting Roszkow," Max cautioned himself. He actually had come to Poland for that reason alone.

"Reyzl," he said, "I came to Poland to visit my parents' graves. I will not leave here without going to Roszkow."

"You came to Poland to see me. I'm your grave," she said with a tantalizing smile.

"You'll have to go with me to Roszkow."

"I'm ready to go with you to the ends of the earth."

"What will happen to Basha?"

"Wait, my dear. I've thought everything through. We'll take her with us. Rich people travel with a maid. Of course, if you're so inclined, she can help you, too," said Reyzl, laughing and winking.

"What are we doing after breakfast?"

"Give me your passport."

Max became apprehensive. "My passport? Why do you need my passport?"

"Last night you gave your sacred word that you would trust me. You said I am the general and you are the plain soldier."

"Still—"

"Don't you see that we need two passports, for a husband and wife or for a sister and brother. It can be done either way. I know a forger who can make ten or one hundred passports, as many as you want. He's a good friend of mine and also doesn't ask any questions."

"Does he know Spanish?"

"He knows everything, even Turkish. Don't be afraid. He won't ruin your passport. He'll just make a copy and write in my name. Shmuel gives him a lot of work to do. He once had a factory for counterfeiting three-ruble notes. If some ninny hadn't squealed on him, he would be another Rothschild today. He served five years in Makatow."

"When would I get a passport back? Without a passport, I'm a dead man."

"In a few days. You can rest easy, Max. Come, wash up and we'll eat breakfast. We have a lot to do yet and the day doesn't stand still. Shmuel could come back any day now and it's not a good idea for him to see you. I'll tell him that you went away and I don't know where."

"You're afraid of him, then?"

"I care as much about him as I do about last year's frost. But I don't want him to start blabbing. Pardon me, but you are too softhearted. You can't have any pity. My uncle used to say, 'Making a living is war.' And that's how it is with everything. If you can't stand the smell of gunpowder, don't go to war. He's had me for twelve years and that's enough. He doesn't need a lover anymore. Of course, he doesn't want to lose me, but he can't force me to stay either. I'll have them make a passport for you in a different name and you can move into another hotel. You can wait there until I'm ready. I have to sell the furniture, bag and baggage. He'll make a fuss, but I can handle him. He's not the only one who is buddy-buddy with the police." And Reyzl Kork winked.

"She swore falsely yesterday," Max said to himself. "Compared to her, Rochelle is a saint. Oh, Mama, I'm sinking into filth up to my neck!" Max chewed the fresh bagel and thought that if Reyzl took his passport, he would be in her hands. And yet he knew he would give her the passport. He would have to rely on her entirely. Reyzl handed him another bagel spread with butter and cottage cheese and poured him a cup of coffee. In his years with Rochelle he had become unused to underworld women. He had dreamed only of daughters of the rich, princesses and fine ladies. But Reyzl had dragged him back to the swamp. Her black eyes reflected a smile of womanly satisfaction and the complacency of evildoers who are never punished and always rewarded. "Wait, Reyzele," Max said to himself. "You'll singe your wings on me."

Unexpectedly he said aloud, "Do you have a photograph of your parents?"

Reyzl stopped chewing. "What's this? No, my dear. I don't have one. My mother, God forbid, never even looked at a man. Who took photographs in those days? Not proper folk."

Max had returned to the Hotel Bristol. He was to wait until Reyzl returned his passport, she having promised that her forger would speed it up. She wanted to sell off all the things in her apartment and find customers to buy her household goods. She said everything had to be done very quickly, before Shmuel Smetena returned from Lodz.

In the hotel lobby he was handed a letter with many postal markings and Argentine stamps. Rochelle's letter had been sent to Paris and forwarded from there. It was dated six weeks back. Rochelle's handwriting was an almost undecipherable scrawl, but one thing was clear. She was angry and even mentioned the word divorce.

When Rochelle had married him, she didn't know how to read and write. Later she had hired a teacher and taken lessons for several years. In comparison with Rochelle, Max was virtually an author. He had learned how to write in Roszkow, teaching himself by reading newspapers and dime novels. He picked up modern expressions from the Yiddish theater and from listening to lecturers. He had even taken the floor at a meeting of the Burial Society. Reading the letter over and over again, Max learned that Rochelle had been suffering from eczema, that she was having trouble with her Spanish maid Rosita, that it was cold and rainy in Argentina, and when was Max coming home?

"Yes, when and what for?" Max asked himself.

There were several words in the letter that Max simply could not make out. He picked it up again and tried once more. Suddenly he deciphered the word "anniversary," and instantly understood the whole sentence: "It will soon be the anniversary of Arturo's death."

"God in heaven, how could I have forgotten?" Three weeks ago it had been two years since Arturo's death.

Max sat in silence. Arturo was rotting in the earth while he was planning a prostitution ring with Reyzl. "Should I fast today?" it suddenly occurred to him. But who would gain from his fasting?

Max remembered the séance at the Shkolnikovs'. Arturo did not know a word of Polish, yet it seemed to Max that he had heard Arturo's voice. And what did he mean by saying he wasn't alone in the other world, that he had met *zeyde-bobe*?

In that moment Max made a decision. He would no longer put off his trip to Roszkow. He should have gone as soon as he had arrived in Poland. He was simply afraid to go near the city where he had relatives among the dead and the living.

How can a person be so selfish, so involved with himself? What do they call it? Egotistical. Even savages and thieves have family feelings. "Am I a complete scoundrel?" he said to himself.

There was knocking at his door. A maid came in and said, "You are being called to the telephone."

"Who is it?"

"Madame Theresa."

"Theresa?" Max couldn't recall a woman with that name. "It must be a mistake," he said. Nevertheless, he got up and went out into the corridor to the telephone. The voice sounded familiar, yet strange. She spoke in Polish.

"It's hard for me to speak in Polish," Max said. "Who are you?"

"I'm Theresa Shkolnikov from Dluga Street."

"Oh, the medium!"

"Yes, that's me."

"How did you get my address?"

"My brother gave it to me."

"You must be wondering why I've not been coming to those . . . what do you call them? I've been extremely busy. But tell me why you're calling—has something happened?"

"You were supposed to come to the séance. We had a very successful session. Extraordinary! Your son was trying to make contact with you."

"My son? Contact?"

"Yes, he tried to get in touch with you."

"A minute before you rang I was thinking of him."

"Really? That's remarkable. Thoughts are communicated. My brother asked for you. We were all waiting."

"Perhaps I can come this evening," Max suggested.

"Tonight we don't have a séance, but I would like to talk to you. I have some important things to tell you."

"Perhaps you can come here. May I invite you to supper? Although you're a girl who walks in the heavens, surely you must eat."

"Certainly I eat. Even those who have left this earth eat, although theirs is a different kind of nourishment."

"You mean to tell me that the dead eat?" Max asked.

"Yes, it's a different kind of food."

"I'll give you food for the living," Max retorted, surprised at his own cheerful mood.

Theresa asked, "Where can we meet?"

"Here in my hotel, if you wish."

"Perhaps outside?"

"You can meet me in front of my hotel. Would eight o'clock be good?"

"I'll be there at eight o'clock in front of the Hotel Bristol."

"Good. We'll go somewhere and talk."

How strange. Almost every time when it looked as if he would have to spend a day alone, something came up. He was a bit afraid of this Theresa. Well, if she was such a witch and could speak with the dead, why was she afraid to come to him in his hotel? "I won't start any funny business with her. With such a one it could be terrible."

Max returned to his room. "The devils are playing with me." Was it like this with everyone, or was he a special target? He sat in a chair, lit a cigarette, blowing smoke rings. He had met a man on the ship who said he didn't believe in God. He ate no meat or fish, just fruit and vegetables. He didn't wear a coat or hat even in the worst rain or cold. He told Max that he lived in Montevideo, bathed in the sea every day, and had never yet lived with a woman. He had long hair down to his shoulders and an unkempt beard. During the journey he tried to convince Max that there is no God; everything is nature. He was going to London for some kind of conference with like-minded people. But if everything was nature, why did nature play such tricks? And who created the world, who had filled the sea with so much water, who had cast the boulders on the mountains? And why does the heart beat? Can one nature watch over so many hearts beating at the same time?

Max heard the telephone ringing in the corridor and knew for a certainty it was for him. Then the maid called, "It's for you!"

Max went to the telephone and it was Reyzl Kork.

"Max," she said. "Shmuel Smetena had a stroke!"

"Dead?"

"No, he's alive. They brought him to Warsaw and he asked to be taken to me."

"In that case all our plans are off."

"You must have patience."

"Can he talk?"

"Yes, he even asked for you. They wanted to take him to the hospital but he refused to go. If he's going to die, he said, then it will be here with me. The doctor just left. I've had some day. His mouth is twisted and you can barely understand what he says. Max, it's not the same Shmuel!"

"He has a wife."

"She's in Michalin, in the country. Max, I want you to come over."

"When? Not today."

"All right, come tomorrow. I never figured on such a calamity. They didn't even telephone. When they knocked on the door, I opened it and four men were carrying a bed in which lay Shmuel. If I didn't drop dead of fright then, I'll live forever."

Max was in the mood to eat dinner with someone and regretted he hadn't invited Theresa to join him for dinner, but it was too late to change that. He walked along New World Street until he came to a restaurant. He ordered a *kapushnyok*, cabbage soup, and a Wiener schnitzel.

Well, so Shmuel Smetena had a stroke. Did God do this to Reyzl so she couldn't go with him? Had someone informed Shmuel that his girlfriend was unfaithful and caused the stroke? There was nothing left to do but eat this Polish cabbage (most probably fried in lard) and ruminate over his own fate.

That morning Max had purchased a Yiddish newspaper which he now spread on the table. Immediately he heard mumblings and grumblings. The Poles who ate there threw angry glances at him. He heard the word *zhid*. To the rabbi, Max was a goy, but to these Gentiles he was a Jew. They hated the sight of the Yiddish newspaper. "Let them drop dead. I'm not from here. I'm an American. They can't do anything to me." Max was possessed by a love for this Yiddish newspaper that carried news about Jews and the Jewish situation and made mincemeat out of the anti-Semites.

Max spread his newspaper over the entire table. What month was it? Had the ninth day of Ab already passed? Max remembered the three weeks of mourning, the nine days, the seventeenth day of Tammuz. "On what dates do those holy days fall? I must buy a Jewish calendar!" Then he remembered that this newspaper would have a Jewish date. He turned to the front page and it was the month of Ab. The ninth day of Ab had already passed. It was getting close to the month of Elul. In less than six weeks' time, it would be Rosh Hashanah.

All these years Max had been eating food that was *treyf*. It wasn't all that easy to find kosher meat in Buenos Aires, but now he suddenly felt ashamed for not eating kosher. As long as they hate the Jews, then one might as well be a Jew. Nevertheless, Max ate the cutlet and ordered dessert.

He walked aimlessly along the streets until he came to Grzybowska, where he bought a Jewish calendar. After that he returned to the hotel. It was still several hours until his eight o'clock meeting with Theresa.

He began to read the Yiddish newspaper once again. Among the ads there was one which read: "For rent, a room with all conveniences. Only for a gentleman, No. 3 Dzika Street." A telephone number was listed.

Maybe I should telephone them? Max mused. Why do they want a gentleman? They probably have a daughter to marry off. He knew that it was foolish, but he went into the corridor and called. It's all because I'm lonely, Max justified himself.

When he heard a man's voice, he asked, "Do you have a room to rent?"

"Yes, the rent is ten rubles a month." The voice was not coarse, but a bit thin like that of an older person. The accent was not Warsaw but from the provinces.

"Is it a nice room?" Max asked.

"Nice? It's a salon. It has two windows facing the street and a balcony. For whom do you want the room, for yourself?"

"Yes."

"Please pardon me, but what is your occupation?"

"I'm a foreigner here. I just came from America."

"America? And you want to remain here?"

"No, just for a few weeks."

"We want someone who will stay here, someone stable," he said. "We had a merchant living here for three years, a traveling salesman. He was on the road a lot, but now he has to go to Russia. We are looking for just such a boarder. A fine person. He became like one of the family."

"I have family in Roszkow," Max said, "but I have to be in Warsaw for several weeks."

"That's not for us. We need someone from here, not a stranger."

"Well, that's too bad," said Max. "Have a good summer." He was about to hang up when he heard sounds of bickering and a woman's voice.

"Excuse me, this is Mrs. Parisover. My husband doesn't know about renting rooms. What is it you want? Did you read the ad?"

"Yes, the ad. But your husband—is that your husband?—said that he needs to have someone local, who will stay. As the saying goes, I'm a guest for a while."

"A guest is most welcome. It will be very hard to find someone like we just had—a young man with all the right credentials. The children were crazy about him. But as they say, nothing is forever. He suddenly got another job and had to move. How long are you planning to stay in Warsaw?"

"A few weeks."

"Then you're going back to America?"

"To Argentina."

"Anyway, we won't get someone for the summer," the woman said after some hesitation. "Come over. You'll have a beautiful room here. You won't find anything nicer, not even on Marshalkowska Street."

"Good. I'll take a droshky and come right over."

"I'll be waiting for you."

"What am I doing? What's the good of it to me?" Max asked himself. He knew the answer: he would avoid spending those few hours until eight o'clock alone. He took a droshky and went by way of Miodowa Street, Dluga, and Nalewki. The house was on the corner of Dzika and Nowolipki Streets. Apparently rich people lived here. The steps were clean and on the doors were brass plates with the names of the tenants. Max rang Nathan Parisover's bell. A woman who appeared to be in her late forties or fifties came to the door. Her glistening black eyes had bags under them, her skin was white, and she had the beginning of a double chin. One could see by the regularity of her features that she had once been a beauty. She looked Max up and down from head to toe.

"Well, come in."

She showed Max the room. It had a parquet floor, a bed, a sofa, a desk, and a dry sink. Everything sparkled and shone. Glass doors opened onto a balcony. Max went out and looked at the stores across the street—a delicatessen, spice store, barbershop and a little restaurant. The street was swarming with passersby, all Jews. Droshkies and open wagons were spread out along the cobblestone streets, and from time to time even a truck came through. Young men were shouting and girls were laughing. Palestine, thought Max.

He had a desire to stay there. The street reminded him a little of the Jewish quarters on Corrientes Street in Buenos Aires. But here Jews wore their own style of dress and you heard only one language, Yiddish.

"What would be wrong if I lived here? I could sit for days on the balcony and look out." Still, alone wouldn't be good. He'd have to have someone. Basha? Not for a wife. Reyzl Kork? Not in such a house. These were a different kind of Jew, not the underworld, but respectable people.

Max stood there and stared. He had lived a good part of his life among the lower classes. Every time he tried to pick himself up, something knocked him down again.

"How do you like the room?" said Mrs. Parisover.

"Beautiful," said Max.

"Where are you living now?"

"In the Hotel Bristol."

"Is that so? But a hotel isn't a home. Come, I'll show you the rest of the house." She took him into the living room, dining room, and bedrooms. On all the doorposts there were mezuzahs in wooden cases. The house was imbued with a deep-rooted Jewishness.

A young girl appeared wearing a long, narrow dress with a slit on the side, as was then the fashion. She had large black eyes, a crooked nose, and a high bosom.

The mother seemed almost embarrassed by this ugly daughter and she said. "This is Ruzhke, my youngest. She just graduated from high school. She knows Hebrew."

"Mama, are you starting up again?"

"What am I doing? It cost us a fortune but we believe in education. Money you can lose, but if you have knowledge in your head, it stays. Have you heard of the Havatselet School?"

"Yes, I think so."

"We have two other daughters. One is married. The wedding was this winter. It cost us a mint, but thank God she got a wonderful husband, a bookkeeper. He knows the Torah, too. My other daughter has a job in a shop on Miodowa Street. They both went to school, but we put all our energy into the younger one. May God send her a suitable match. That's all we want."

"Mama, this man just walked in and you start telling him our whole history."

"Well, so he'll live here and become one of the family. What am I actually saying? Parents want to have pleasure from their children. Is that wrong?"

"No, it's not wrong," said Max. "What else do we have children for?"

"What's your name?"

"Max Barabander."

"Do you have children, Panye Barabander?"

Max was silent for a while.

"I had a wife, I had a son, but God took them away."

"What? God spare us from such misfortune," and Mrs. Parisover wrung her hands.

"Nothing remains. That's why I came here. I hoped that the trip would help me a little."

"Where do you live?"

"In Buenos Aires."

"So far away? Well, it's a big world. What can you do? Everything is fated. But as long as you are alive, you can't kill yourself. You're still young. You'll probably marry and have other children."

"That's very little comfort."

The girl with the wild black eyes and the crooked nose said, "In Argentina it's winter now, isn't it?"

"Yes, when it's summer here, it's winter there."

"She knows everything. She studies books, every detail. When do you want to move in?"

"I'll pay you for a month and I'll move in not before the day after tomorrow."

"Well, as you wish. Why live in the Hotel Bristol when you have a room here? It's expensive there."

"Here are your ten rubles."

The woman looked at the banknote and said, "Let it be with *mazel*. Do you have many things?"

"Two valises."

"Bring them here. We'll take care of you like our own child."

When Max Barabander approached the Hotel Bristol at five minutes to eight, Theresa was waiting outside. He had recognized her from a distance, tall, thin, wearing a straight dress and a hat with a veil. She looked a lot older than she had in the apartment on Dluga Street. Evidently she was impatient, because she kept turning her head first to the left, then to the right. She had an unusually long neck, Max observed, reminding him of one of the exotic birds in the zoological garden. When she saw him, she began to tremble.

Max went over to her. Taking off his Panama hat he kissed Theresa's hand over her long glove.

"Where can we go?" she asked.

"Not far from here there's a coffee shop. We'll eat supper there."

"I'm not hungry," she said, "but I can have a cup of coffee. I know it wasn't tactful on my part to call you, but I'm in a difficult spot, and as my mother used to say, 'When you're drowning you clutch at a straw.'"

"What's happened?"

"We'll talk when we sit down. Perhaps you can find a separate table where people can't hear. Naturally everybody here in Warsaw knows me from the séances. Also, my picture was in the newspaper. But I don't think they will recognize me. I have short hair, as you know, but I've pinned on a braid and covered my face."

"Yes, you look different, older. You speak Yiddish well. I thought you spoke only Polish."

"My father was a religious Jew, a Hasid. We place our advertisements in the Yiddish newspaper and I read *Haynt* every day and *Moment*, and naturally the Polish gazettes, too."

"How did you become a medium?"

"I'll tell you everything. But first of all I must tell you that Bernard Shkolnikov is not my brother."

"I guessed that myself."

"How come?"

"Oh, he's small and you're tall, and he seems to be about thirty years older than you. He's your lover."

"Please, not so loud. People are listening. Where is the coffeehouse?"

"Here, across the street."

"That's good."

In the café Max found a table near a window, away from the other tables. Except for a Polish squire who was sitting in the opposite corner reading a newspaper with a magnifying glass, nobody else was there. Max and Theresa sat down.

A waitress appeared immediately. She was wearing a purple dress and a short apron with a bow on the side. She looked young, about eighteen, fresh from the country. Like a plum still covered with dew, Max thought. She wouldn't be poison either.

Shaking her head as if to say "Men will be men," Theresa gave him a look in which there was both accusation and understanding. She ordered a cup of cocoa and Max a roll, herring, and an omelet. When the waitress left, Max said, "From a cup of cocoa you won't get the strength to bring over spirits."

"Don't make jokes. There are spirits."

"Where are they?"

"Everywhere."

"Have you yourself seen them?"

"Not once but thousands of times."

"What do they look like?"

"Oh, I don't want to get into such a discussion. They don't look like the dead, they look like the living. There are no dead."

"Who's buried in the cemetery?"

"Pieces of clay."

"Please tell me more. Since I lost my son, I think about such things day and night."

"It's impossible to discuss."

"My son doesn't know any Polish, yet during the séance he spoke to me in Polish. He said that he met his grandparents. Where did he meet them?"

"I don't know. I hear certain words and I repeat them. Sometimes I don't even hear words; I just get a certain impression. Spirits don't always use language. They give you a message and you know what they have communicated."

"Why don't they communicate with me?"

"I don't know. You have to be born with a talent for receiving messages. Once, I went to a hairdresser to get a haircut. I'm not comfortable in long hair. I was sitting on a chair and she was standing over me with the scissors when suddenly there was a knocking. It sounded like someone banging on the wooden chair with a hammer, but somehow it came from within. I can't even describe it. Knocking is a sign that—how shall I put it?— someone wants my attention. Usually such things don't happen when I'm out. But this time there was this rapping on the hairdresser's chair. 'I don't know who you are,' she said to me, 'but do me a favor and go away. I'm afraid of such things.' I tried to pay her but she wouldn't take any money. She simply threw me out."

"Perhaps you can make something knock in my house. I won't throw you out."

"I can't make anything happen. If it happens, it happens."

"What did the spirit want? The one that was knocking at the hairdresser's."

"I don't know. At the hairdresser's the raps came as if the spirit was ready to tear the house down. But when I got home I didn't hear from it anymore. The spirits are like the living. They have their whims and craziness."

"Where are they? What do they do the whole day?"

"I don't know. They're somewhere and they don't give me a report. Once, I was sitting in the house darning a sock and suddenly I saw an army, a whole army. They weren't troops of our time but of another time, perhaps from thousands of years ago. They were wearing plates of armor and carrying spears. Some were riding horses, others chariots. Thousands of soldiers passed by on a road with horses, donkeys, and other animals, too. It took about three-quarters of an hour before they were gone. If you were to ask if I saw Romans, Egyptians, or Greeks, I couldn't say. They surely weren't Jews."

"Are you saying armies that have long since died are marching in heaven?"

"Not in heaven. I saw them here on earth."

"Where were they going? On maneuvers?"

"I don't know."

"You dreamed it. That's all."

"Let it be as you say. I don't get rich if you believe me, or poor if you don't believe me."

"Excuse me, but that's your livelihood."

"I'm not a cripple, I can earn my bread. I'm not that ugly either. I could marry and my husband would make a living for me. I never wanted to use this power of mine for practical purposes. I telephoned you and you still don't know why. I didn't come to boast of my talents. My situation is like this. I must leave." And Theresa's tone of voice altered. "Bernard told me that you are a rich man. Perhaps you could help me? I don't mean with money, but help me to tear myself away from here." Both were silent, and Theresa took a sip of her cocoa.

"Why must you leave?"

"Bernard has virtually enslaved me. That's what it is. He discovered these powers in me and helped me develop, but I have paid him back God knows how many times. Besides that, he doesn't let anyone come near me. The story is like this: There's a man here called Klusky, not a Jew, who's also a medium. He's the follower of a certain Professor Akhorovich.

I'm in a dilemma. From most people who come to ask about a robbery or a husband who ran away, you cannot make enough for the Sabbath, as they say. We have one rich client from a very well-known family, Duke Sapieha, who lost his wife. He loved her passionately, almost to madness or worse. In the beginning he went to Klusky, who brought him all kinds of greetings from her. But for Sapieha that wasn't enough. When Klusky brought him to me, I received impressions of his wife many times and even visions. But that was not enough for him. In brief, it became clear that the duke wanted the impossible—a materialization. That's what we call it when a spirit becomes embodied and appears in human form. Such things seldom happen. You can count them on the fingers of one hand. It's not easy for a spirit to become corporeal. But Adam Sapieha was insistent. I want to be completely forthright: you can't be totally honest in this professioin and it's entirely the fault of the clients. For them an evening without a contact is a swindle; they always have to get their money's worth. But the human soul isn't a mechanical thing. You just can't pick up a telephone receiver and dial someone on the other side. But those who pay their three rubles demand it. A situation is created where, if you can't tell them the truth, then you must fool them. Most people are satisfied with lies. They actually demand it."

"It wasn't Arturo, then?"

"I don't know. Sometimes I myself don't know. I also don't know why I'm telling you all this. You're a stranger and you're leaving soon. I myself don't have anything to fear. I spoke with Professor Akhorovich. He tested me, had a whole series of séances with me, and declared publicly that I possess extraordinary powers. He also said no medium could call up Duke Sapieha's wife every night."

"And what did you do? You yourself became his wife?"

Theresa looked up. "Yes, how did you guess?"

"Oh, I was once a thief. I know how you fool a sucker."

"A thief? Where?"

"Here in Warsaw."

"Really? Everything is possible. I've been put in the position of having to appear before the duke twice a week. He's not satisfied with talk. He embraces me, presses me against him, holds me tight, tries to get near me. It has begun to feel like prostitution, and Bernard is driving me to it. Aside from the fact that the duke pays good money, he's also a drunk and half crazy. He's already threatened to shoot Bernard. He's even put a revolver to my breast. Can you believe that an infatuated husband threatens the ghost of his wife with a revolver? That's what human madness can bring you to."

"He knows that it's you and not his wife."

"Yes, of course he knows, but he insists on fooling himself. I can't bear it anymore. I must run away. If not, I'll have to kill myself."

It grew dark outside and electric lights came on. Warm winds blew in through an open vent. Max realized that the days were getting shorter and the month of Elul was approaching, when Jews say their penitential prayers and even fish in the waters are said to tremble.

Theresa had become hungry and Max ordered a roll and herring and eggs for her. He watched her eating and thought, She can't eat ghosts; she has to fill her belly with food like everyone else. Could she fit into my plan? he wondered.

Now that Shmuel Smetena was sick and Reyzl Kork had put everything on hold, the whole project was in abeyance. He had lost Tsirele. Reyzl had control over Basha. Shmuel could linger on for weeks, even years. Max frowned and knit his brows.

"So you want to run away from that crazy squire and also from Shkolnikov?"

"From everyone and everything."

"What do you want to do in Argentina? Get married?"

"Whatever I want to do, it's without partners."

"You don't love Skholnikov anymore?"

"I'm simply his plaything. He uses me, that's all. He thinks he knows everything and loves to give advice. I heard how he talked to you about hypnotism and messages. He himself is half crazy; he goes to neurologists. That's the truth. He's made me sick, too. If I don't tear myself away from him, I'll have a nervous breakdown."

"What can I do for you?"

"I can't apply for an overseas passport because if he finds out he'll make a row. He pushes me at Sapieha and at the same time he's madly jealous. How old do you think he is?"

"He looks about fifty."

"Fifty-eight. I'll have to pack a small bag and steal across the border. I thought you could help me."

"Crossing the border is a small matter. But what about afterward? Do you have money for expenses?"

"I have a little money. How much does it cost to sail to Argentina?"

"You can't give away your last groschen for a ship ticket. When you get there, you can't begin your business with the spirits the very next morning. You have to get to know people. In Argentina a woman can't walk alone on the street. The police won't protect you, because if you're going about without a chaperone, then you're a streetwalker."

Theresa looked up from her plate. "Is that how it is there? How is it in America? I mean in New York."

"A woman alone is like a ship without a rudder everywhere."

"Hm. That's why Bernard has such power over me. I can't place an ad in the newspapers by myself. I can't even rent an apartment by myself. How long will women be enslaved like this? I hear that abroad it's different."

"It's not different. In London there was a demonstration and a woman tried to defeat the Minister because women want equal rights, but it was useless. If a man doesn't accompany you, then you have to have a servant or your mother. Otherwise they won't even let you into a hotel. How is it with the ghosts? Do the women there have equal rights?"

"Oh, you're making fun of me!"

"I'm not laughing. I'm asking. As long as ghosts eat and talk, then they're like people. Seriously, in Argentina it's worse than here. In Argentina there are also fortune-tellers. I once went to see one of them and she foretold my future. But she was an old woman and a native. I don't have to tell you that you'll have to learn Spanish. Jews seldom turn to fortune-tellers, and then how many Jews are there? You must know Spanish. In your profession you have to charm them with words. What languages do you know besides Yiddish and Polish?"

"Russian."

"Any others?"

"None."

"Wherever you go, you must learn the language. You must be able to rattle on. Have you ever heard how gypsies talk?"

"Please don't compare me with them. I came to you hoping that you could help me. Instead, you are making my heart sink."

"I'm telling you the truth. Unless you want me to deceive you."

"I don't have to be a medium."

"Whatever you want to do, you have to learn the language. If you work in a factory, your earnings won't be worth talking about. Jewish women don't work in Argentina. In New York it's different. There you'll go to work in a *landsman*'s factory or somewhere else and no one will bother you. I was there and I know the city. But it's bad there, too. You'll have to be a servant for a missus—that's what they call the mistresses—and you'll sleep with three other girls in one room. You'll work a whole week and you'll have barely enough for a piece of bread. You'll have to go to work by train and come home by train. In winter you'll freeze from the cold and in summer you'll be suffocated by the heat."

"That means there's no way out for me."

"You must be someone's wife or someone's lover."

Theresa lifted her glass as if to drink and then put it down again. "To be someone's wife or lover, I must find that person appealing. I can't sell myself like a piece of merchandise in the marketplace."

"Some can and some can't. Among the Turks a man buys a wife and nobody considers it a sin. The father sells his daughters. Our own ancestor Jacob bought Rachel from Laban for seven years' work and swindled him in the bargain."

"I don't have a father to sell me."

"Come with me. I'm looking for a lover."

Max was nonplused by his own words. He was afraid that Theresa would berate him or even get up from the table and leave. She sat still, with her head bowed, and looked at her plate.

Outside, a streetcar had stopped a few steps from the window. Some passengers got off, others got on. As Max looked, he thought, Are all their affairs in order? Or are they as mixed up as Theresa and I are? The streetcar bell rang and it glided away. Where the rod touched the overhead wires, electric sparks flashed.

Theresa lifted her head. "You're making fun of me."

"I'm not. I have a wife who is sick and half crazy. I can't live with her anymore."

"From what you said to Bernard, you can't live with anyone."

"If I had someone I could feel close to, I would. At my age it's hard to run from one woman to the other. I'm looking for a close relationship, a friend." This is actually the opposite of my entire plan, Max thought. I'm turning everything upside down.

He sat there amazed at his own words, and even more amazed that Theresa was listening to him. He had realized for years that no matter how unreasonable an idea might be, or how wild his words sounded even to himself, people nevertheless listened to him. He had actually proposed that Theresa become his lover and had done so without knowing whether he liked her. At the same time, he feared that she might not consent. "Was it because of her that I rented a room at the Parisovers'?" He relied completely on his tongue, which was his ruler and his destiny.

He heard Theresa say, "We hardly know each other. First we'll have to get acquainted."

"We'll get acquainted. What you told me about yourself is interesting. Were you ever in love with Bernard Shkolnikov?"

"Oh, he's so much older than I. He discovered my gifts, taught me. He was my teacher and my father. I come from a small town in western Poland. It couldn't have been otherwise. I became his mistress."

"Why not his wife?"

"He has a wife who doesn't want to divorce him."

"The old story."

"But how long can it last? He's almost sixty and I'm not even thirty-three. He forces me to act out all those deceptions with Duke Sapieha. That means there's no more love from his side either. He simply wants to use me, sell me, and keep the money for himself. He never tells me how much he has, even though I helped him earn it. I don't get anything more out of him than my food and sometimes a dress. I don't wish him anything bad, but what would I do if something happened to him? His wife would come and throw me out. He was once ill and things looked bad. Thank God, he got better. I watched over him day and night. But they told me that his wife had sent her emissaries to see how he was doing."

"He doesn't have a will?"

"I once dared to mention such a word and he hit me."

"So."

"I simply want to run away. If I don't run away from him, he'll get me back. That's what he's like."

"In other words, he's hypnotized you."

"He can move a stone."

"Perhaps you love him?"

"Even if I do, I have to run away."

"Come to me. I also have a wife. But I'll sign over a house to you or whatever you want. I'll hire a teacher for you and you'll learn Spanish. It's not a difficult language. You'll open a salon and the money will go to you, not me. I don't need your money."

"What will your wife say?"

"She can't say anything. Everyone in Argentina has a mistress, even priests. Such women are looked on with respect. I've been left without a child and I would want a son to say Kaddish after me. To whom should I leave my fortune? You're still young and surely would also want to have a child."

"Yes, I love children. As long as we're living as sister and brother—he introduces me to everyone as his sister—there's no possibility of having his child. I became pregnant twice and had to go to a midwife for an abortion. The second time I began to hemorrhage and almost died."

"That's no life for a young woman." It became quiet. Another trolley stopped, entirely empty. How strange.

"When are you going?" Theresa asked.

"I can go tomorrow. There's nothing stopping me. I've done some foolish things. There's only one thing that I still want to do, visit the little town where I come from. Roszkow is its name. I have relatives there and I would like to see them. I got homesick for Warsaw. Maybe it was fated that I should meet you. If you want, pack a few things, or don't pack anything, I don't care, and we'll go together to Roszkow and from there to the border."

"Whereabouts in Roszkow?"

"It's not far from the border."

"What will I do in Roszkow?"

"You'll wait for me for a few days. The truth is that I didn't go there because I feel lonely traveling by myself. Since my son passed away, I can't remain alone for a minute. I'm possessed by melancholy and I want to make an end of it."

"Is that how much you loved him?"

"I don't know if I loved him that much. Everything became empty, terribly empty. Do you believe that the dead live?"

"Either the dead live, or the living are dead."

"Well, you're an interesting girl. I feel I could be happy with you."

ow crazy can a person be?" Max said to himself. He had paid ten rubles for a room on Dzika Street and he was still living in the Hotel Bristol. Theresa was ready to go around the world with him. She had said so plainly, she would accompany him wherever he wanted to go. But Reyzl Kork had his passport. He had telephoned her several times every day. She either didn't answer, or if she did, she explained, "I can't go to the forger right now. I can't leave a sick man alone."

Max paced back and forth in his room. Why had he given his passport to a whore on Krochmalna Street? Should he notify the police, should he put a revolver to her breast? She had her thugs. They would beat him up and he would get arrested. There must be an Argentinian consul somewhere, but how would he explain giving away his passport? "Well, I walked into a trap."

Max tried to telephone Basha, but her mistress answered the phone. "Basha is busy," she screamed, and banged down the receiver.

"I deserve a beating," Max said to himself. "I deserve everything that happens to me. The rabbi has cursed me."

Without the passport Max couldn't even go to Roszkow. Gendarmes come to your train compartment and ask to see your passport. If you don't have one, you're arrested and sent away in a procession of convicts to Siberia.

Having been born in Roszkow, he could get his birth certificate there for a new passport, but how to visit Roszkow?

"I'll shoot her. I'll shoot her and then put a gun to my head," Max said to himself. "Anything is better than rotting in prison."

He went out into the corridor once more and rang Reyzl. A man came to the telephone and answered in a rough voice.

"Does Reyzl Kork live here?"

"Yes, what do you want?"

"I have to talk to her."

"What's your name?"

"Max Barabander."

"Barabander, eh? Wait a minute."

He went for Reyzl, but after five minutes passed and nothing happened, Max hung up. When he phoned again, there was no answer. He telephoned a third and a fourth time without success. Could Reyzl have found out about his meeting with Theresa? Had she sent spies after him? Or did she simply need his passport for her dirty business?

"Shooting her is not enough. I'll flay her alive. She'll be happy when I finish her off."

It was years since he had found himself in such a rage. His boyhood fantasies of shooting, beating, and stabbing had ceased. All his adult thoughts had been focused on women, on his health, spas, and hydrotherapy. But now Max's blood was seething with anger. He opened his valise, took out the revolver, and counted the bullets.

No, I have to buy a knife, he decided. He would get one at the market stalls or from a peddler at the Iron Gate, where he could speak Yiddish.

Well, that's my luck, he thought. He remembered his dream of sitting in jail, where the prisoners were staring at him silently. That dream had always terrified him. He always awoke from it with a strange heaviness, and the certainty he was being shown God's plans, as in the dream of the Pharaoh of Egypt. "What was the name of the chief of the bakers to whom Joseph revealed his dreams?" Max asked himself, remembering the words: "And the birds shall eat thy flesh." He saw the scene just as he had pictured it in cheder—a half-dark dungeon, a long-haired Joseph in a torn shirt, the chief butler and the chief baker.

"God will lift up your head and return you to your position . . ."

"Pharaoh will chop off your head and hang your body from a tree."

He still remembered the exegetical explanation of the text in the Torah: "And I, when I came from Padanaram". . . . "And even though I have imposed on you the burden of my burial, although I did not do so for your mother Rachel . . . There was still a little land to plow . . . The earth was full of holes like a sieve . . ." Max tried to recall the words that followed, but he could remember no more. Only the melody remained.

"What was my teacher's name? Itchele Chentshiner. How long ago? Well, no matter, I'm lost, lost. I won't escape my fate." Max put the revolver in his pocket. He went downstairs, leaving his key with the clerk. Silently Max said goodbye to the hotel, the clerk, and all the staff. "Tonight I'll surely be lying dead somewhere. Forgive me, Rochelle; forgive me, Tsirele; forgive me, Rabbi. I deserve everything, but I hope at least they bury me in a Jewish cemetery."

Max walked by way of Theater Square, Senatorska Street, and Bankowy Square. The clock in the Council House showed ten minutes after two. Up in the tower, so high that you had to crane your neck, was the little figure of a fireman who was inspecting the building. An open wagon with stage sets that showed painted houses, a garden, a lake, and swans was being driven to the opera house.

On Bankowy Square a van carrying money drove through the Iron Gate, protected by two armed guards. Max stared at them and they stared back. "What would happen if I took out my revolver and shot them? I would be caught, the street is full of police. Well, foolish thoughts. They no doubt are the fathers of children."

Max went into Przechodnia Street and came out between the pillars of Vienna Hall, where market women were calling out: "Buttons, needles, pillowcases, remnants!" But nobody was selling knives.

Where do you get a knife in Warsaw? Max wondered. He had no intention of letting Reyzl die an easy death. He turned into Mirowski Square, heading for the market stalls. There you could get everything, even fish from the sea. He saw butter, all kinds of cheese, many varieties of apples, pears, plums, dates, figs, halvah, and yes, beef, chickens, ducks, turkeys. Well, and what is this? Pheasants, hares, but no knives.

"God, what's happening to me? Maybe there's still time to find a way out. Maybe I'll go to the police and tell them every-thing. You don't get hanged for losing a passport. I'll send Rochelle a telegram and tell her to come. She'll save me."

Max stopped for a while. Between two stalls there were tables displaying pots, faience ware, and china. On one table he saw knives, ordinary kitchen knives with wooden handles, dull as wood. Max picked out the best knife and paid for it. He ran his nail along the edge like a *shoykhet* with his slaughtering knife.

How remarkable that a few steps farther on Max saw an old Gentile with a knife-sharpening machine, a man with white whiskers and sunken cheeks, wearing a blue hat with a shiny visor. Max stopped him and handed him the knife. He had forgotten how to say "sharpen" in Polish, so he used sign language. The old man rolled the machine over to the sidewalk and sharpened the knife on his whetstone. Sparks began to fly, and from time to time he inspected the edge.

"Is this how you commit murder? I'm just fooling around," Max said to himself. He paid the man twenty groschen, and when he tried to make change, Max waved it off.

He now went up to Ciepla Street, passing the barracks of the Woliner Regiment. He heard soldiers marching and drilling in the courtyard. One soldier was riding on a horse. Max stood and stared. He had the feeling he had already lived through this. Awake or in a dream? Everything seemed familiar: the knife grinder, the one-eyed woman who sold him the knife, the sergeant riding around on a horse, while a corporal or a three-striper was calling out commands in Russian. From a distance all the soldiers looked alike and appeared to be wooden dummies. Their bayonets glinted in the sun. Dust arose from under the horses' feet.

"They are learning how to kill people. It seems that people must kill. Sooner or later people become so vile that they must be put away." Once again he became enraged. "If she won't give me the passport, she's dead. She's not going to make a fool out of me. I'm sick of living anyway."

Max came to the corner of Krochmalna Street and went over to the gate at No. 23. "It's not too late to go back home," a voice warned him.

He went up the stairs to Reyzl Kork. He knocked, but no one answered. He pushed on the door and it opened. He passed through the corridor and the center room. He opened a door and there was Shmuel Smetena, sitting in bed with three cushions behind his back, dressed in a maroon bathrobe. His mouth was twisted and there were blue pouches under his eyes. He looked exceptionally heavy and bloated.

For a while, Shmuel looked at Max from under his heavy eyebrows. Then he said, "Well, come in."

"Reyzl isn't here?"

"Went shopping. The maid is away. How did you get in? The door is open?"

"Not closed."

"Well, come in. You know what hit me."

"Yes, I see. Such things pass."

"Ha? I was strong and healthy. Suddenly something in me began to shiver and everything turned black before my eyes. I fell in the middle of the street, among all the wagons and trucks. When I came to, I was lying in the hospital."

"It happens. You don't look bad."

"Lived sixty years and never went to a doctor. Look at my mouth—crooked."

"It'll straighten out."

"I didn't want to stay in the hospital, I hate them. Someone died in the bed next to me. How can you become well when someone expires right near you? Some of the gang came by and I said, 'I don't want to stay in Lodz. I've lived in Warsaw and I'll die in Warsaw.' They brought a folding bed and carted me off to the train. Reyzl knew nothing about it. She opened the door and saw me lying there. She let out a scream that you could hear half a block away."

"Is she taking care of you?"

"Who else would take care of me if not her? I took her out of the garbage heap and made her a queen. She would still be rotting in the gutter if not for me. My wife is somewhere in Michalin, in the country, may the Devil take her. You pull the wagon for years until you fall down. When you have two homes, you can't save. A ruble slips through my fingers, and that's all well and good when you're not sick. If I can't go to the tavern with the lords, they won't come to me."

"Maybe I can help you."

"Help? With what?"

"I could lend you money."

"Why should you do that? You're not going to stay here, you're going away. If you were to stay in Warsaw . . ."

"I'm not going away. When you're yourself again, you'll pay me back."

"Imagine that! My gang dropped dead on me and here comes a stranger from the other side of the world and wants to lend me money. Nowadays a man is worth less than a fly. He lives, and in a moment he's gone."

"You'll live and be well."

"Well, maybe. Reyzl has money. She's saved a bundle. But I don't feel like taking from her. What's the expression? A taker is not a giver. A man gives everything away and doesn't even get a thank you. But if you need something from a woman, it's better to be lying in your grave."

"I'll lend you money. For me you're reliable."

"It's not like it used to be. When I came to Krochmalna Street, girls were being shipped all over the world like cattle. A girl was seduced and right away she became a prostitute. A girl who wasn't a virgin was in deep trouble. Today some girls sell themselves, others want to overthrow the Tsar. No matter what, it's not like it was. She got close to you, eh?"

Max was silent for a while. "Got close? No."

"Why not? She said she fancied you."

"She's not faithful to you, then?"

Shmuel Smetena waited for a while, his mouth becoming even more twisted. "What can you expect with someone like that? She teases. My mother was a virtuous Jewish woman. My father left for five years to serve in the Russian Army and she remained as faithful to him as on the first day. She sewed clothes for him and sent money to him in his regiment. Today they're just riffraff. On Yom Kippur they go to shul. The next morning it's anything goes. Maybe in the other world we'll learn the truth."

"Is there another world?"

"There must be something."

Shmuel Smetena closed his eyes and suddenly Max heard a snore. He had fallen asleep. After a while Max got up and looked around. In the center room he decided to look in the dresser. There was his passport! He was so taken aback, he just stood stock-still. He leafed through it for a while, and put it in his inside pocket. "A miracle!" an inner voice cried. "It wasn't fated that I should kill a human being." Now it became clear to Max that all the talk about a forger and copies had been lies. Reyzl had simply taken his passport to keep him hostage. But why had she left it in the dresser? He was overcome; up in heaven they were not allowing him to perish. He didn't deserve it, but a guardian angel was watching over him. He had to leave the apartment and breathe some fresh air.

At the gate, he saw Reyzl Kork coming toward him with a basket of food and vegetables—a chicken, a head of cabbage, potatoes, tomatoes. When she saw him, she froze.

"Were you upstairs?" she said.

"I came to see how Shmuel is."

"How is he doing? Why didn't you telephone that you were coming?"

"I telephoned and some man answered and said he would fetch you and left me hanging there."

"Who was that? What are you talking about? No one comes to visit here. That was yesterday, not today. It must have been Menashe, the barber-surgeon."

"What happened to my passport?" said Max severely.

"Wait, let me put my basket down. It must weigh a hundred pounds. I've given your passport to the forger, but he's very busy and keeps delaying. With Shmuel in such a state, I don't have time to see the forger. Why are you in need of the passport? You want to leave?"

"Maybe, yes."

"And you'll leave me to sweat it out here?"

"So what. Did I seduce you? Were you just an innocent little virgin?"

Reyzl looked at him half imploringly, half impudently. "You don't need me anymore?"

"First of all, return my passport; then we'll talk."

"The passport is with the forger, not with me."

"Where does he live? I'll go there myself."

"He won't want to talk to you."

"That means I have to stick it out here in Warsaw until you're good and ready."

"Max, what's the matter with you?"

"The matter is that you are a pig, a bitch. It's a good deed to kill a person like you. Killing you is too great an honor for you. You should be squashed like a bedbug."

"Max, have you lost your mind?"

"Whore, bitch, vile liar!"

He could no longer hold himself back. He gave her a resounding smack. Reyzl almost keeled over.

"Max, what are you doing?"

"Here's my passport." Max took the booklet out of his inner pocket and flashed it in front of her face. Reyzl's eyes filled with laughter and pain.

"You looked in my dresser?"

"It was lying right there. The whole business with the forger was a bluff. Liar, thief, crook, leech! Your time has come. I'll lay you out cold." And he clenched his fist.

"Max, don't do anything foolish," Reyzl said quietly, warning him. "If you lay a hand on me again, the street will swarm with people who will take my side."

"Who, your pimps?"

"When you leave here, you won't have a whole bone in your body."

"Drop dead!" and Max spat at her forehead.

Reyzl wiped the spittle off with her sleeve. "Max, you should be ashamed of yourself."

"I should be ashamed of myself? Why did you keep my passport when I asked for it?"

"I was going to bring it to the forger, but Shmuel suffered a stroke. Max dear, why are we standing at the gate? There'll soon be a crowd gathering. Come up and let's talk like human beings."

"*You* a human being? You're less than a worm. It's even disgusting to step on you."

"I am what I am. I never told you I was a rebbetzin. You're the one that's running to the rabbis, not me. You came to me and I was straight with you. If you want to become respectable, that's not my fault. We got together, we agreed, and I thought things were ready to roll. Shmuel was already worn out and now he's finished. This is a house, not a hospice. It's plain and simple. If you'll wait a few days, I'm yours and you can do with me what you will. I didn't want to take away your passport. What do I need it for? I can get a thousand passports to your one. That night you swore by your son's soul that you love me."

"I didn't swear by anyone's soul, liar, bluffer, swindler!"

"You swore! I'm not making it up. You've probably seduced someone else and want to run away with her. Maxele, I won't hold you back. I can't and I don't want to. You don't have to stand here and call me names. If you want to go, go in peace and have a good trip. If I want to see my sister in Argentina, I can go without you. I can pay my way. Everyone on the street runs after me. That's the truth. I could have a boy of nineteen or my name isn't Reyzl. We could be a good pair, but if you hit me now, I can't expect any good from you."

"What should I do? Kiss you?"

"Why not? Come upstairs and do whatever you want with me. I'll get rid of him today or tomorrow, and the whole

world will be open to us. We'll take Basha and she'll be our
servant."

"Why did you see to it that we didn't meet?" Max asked,
surprised at his own words.

"Because you don't know what's the matter with you.
You're doing everything without thinking. Basha came home on
the Sabbath more dead than alive. The old couple won't let her
out of the house now. You don't have to do things that way,
Maxele. You need me more than I need you."

"You're not worth a damn to me."

"Well go, and may God help you."

For a while they both stood still. Reyzl looked at her basket.
Max hesitated.

"You were unfaithful to Shmuel. All your talk was lies,"
he said.

"How do you know I was untrue to him? He hasn't been
a man for three years."

"But you remained a woman, huh?"

"I think I'll remain a woman even when I'm in the grave."

"And the dead bodies will come to you, eh?"

"Meanwhile, I want a live one." And Reyzl picked up her
basket. Max watched as she went into the vestibule, and then
he followed her.

"Give me your basket."

Reyzl's eyes lit up. "You want to be a cavalier? Come, I'll
make you a cup of coffee." He followed, thinking, That's how
an ox goes to slaughter. A bovine heaviness seized him. "Well,
I'm really no better than her," Max said to himself. He touched
his inner pocket. "Everything else, yes, but she won't touch my
passport anymore." Max sat on a bench in the kitchen. Reyzl
put the basket down on the floor.

"Wait, I'll take a look at him."

She went in and lingered a long time. Max took out his pen and began writing numbers in a notebook. It was a week since he had made an accounting of his expenses. "If after all that's happened I go back to her, then I have no character at all," he said to himself. "I'm just a dishrag. Why did I take the room on Dzika Street? I'm simply crazy."

Reyzl returned. "He's sleeping."

"What do you want to do?" Max asked.

"You know what," and she winked.

"There's no viler thing in the whole world," Max said to himself. She opened the door to a bedroom he had never seen before. Reyzl's eyes were full of enticement.

"He could wake up," Max said.

"He can't walk."

"No, Reyzl, I don't want to."

"Don't be an idiot."

"You'll do the same thing to me."

"No, Max, you're a man."

He embraced her and she pressed herself against him. She awoke both lust and hate in him. The telephone rang and Reyzl shook her head from side to side as a sign she wouldn't answer.

Someone knocked on the door and rang the bell.

"Why are they making this racket?" Reyzl said, and her face became flushed as she half kissed and bit him. "Max, we'll go away together?"

"Yes, piece of dirt."

"Don't call me that. I'll be true to you."

She threw herself on the bed and pulled him down on her. The mattress gave a dull thud. She pulled off his jacket, struggled with his pants, his suspenders. His reading glasses fell out of his vest pocket. Suddenly there was a shot and Reyzl screamed. He could smell the stench of gunpowder. Reyzl fell off the bed, picked herself up, and staggered out, shrieking as if possessed, "He shot me! He shot me!"

Max saw blood on the floor. He got up and stared. "Well, this is it, this is it!" he said to himself. Max heard Reyzl screaming, "Help, police! Save me! Save me!" There was a muffled cry from Shmuel Smetena and sounds in the courtyard. Max didn't try to run away. He put his hand in his pocket and the metal of the revolver felt warm. He saw the burnt-out hole in his pocket and realized it could serve as evidence that he had not shot Reyzl intentionally.

Max wanted to take the revolver out of his pocket, but somehow he was afraid to remove this destroyer. He remembered the knife. If they found the knife in his inner pocket, then it would prove that he had come with the intent to commit murder. He had to think quickly, do something to save himself, but everything inside him felt dull and detached. "The rabbi has cursed me!" His head felt heavy, his feet were paralyzed. His spiteful inner enemy had scored a victory. For a while Max forgot what he wanted to do, then he remembered. He bent down to pick up the jacket from the floor, but at that moment the door was thrown open and a policeman, the janitor, and another man rushed in. The police sergeant took his saber from its sheath and shouted, "Hands up!"

Max raised his hands.

He was conveyed in a police wagon to prison. Everything happened precisely as in the dream that had repeated itself so many times. He walked up the iron-clad steps, the heavy door opened, and he entered a room with gray walls and plank beds arranged in rows in the middle. The barred windows, covered with wire mesh, let in little light. In the half-dark, men were standing around in gray jackets and gray pants. Even their faces were gray. They all stared at him in silence. Everything had been ordained from the beginning. Max was seized with a kind of piety mixed with fear. He, Max, had come to Warsaw to perpetrate all this craziness for only one purpose, to realize his dream.